Our Dad is Dead

and Other Fun Things to Talk About

A collection of short stories.

Amanda Hovseth

Giles Hovseth

For information contact:
Synecdoche Publishing
synecdochepublishing.wordpress.com

Cover and Book Design by Amanda Hovseth

Soft Cover ISBN: 978-1-945018-16-9
E-book ISBN: 978-1-945018-09-1
Library of Congress Control Number: 2018915205

1st Edition: 2019

Dedication

To our dad, Dan Hovseth, who was wary of our desire to be writers, but supportive once we were able to prove our abilities. Thank you for raising us to be skeptical dreamers, for teaching us the ability to reason, and training us in the art of wining arguments.

To our mom, Lori Hovseth, who somehow had the strength to raise four children while married to our father. Thank you for always being our greatest supporter and for encouraging us to chase our dreams.

But, most of all, thanks to both of them for introducing us to the lover of the unworthy, forgiver of sins, and Savior of souls, Jesus Christ.

We love you guys,
Amanda and Giles

Story List

"If everyone was 5'11 had brown hair, brown eyes, and was named Dan, the world would be a perfect place."

- *Dan Hovseth (stolen from his brother Bill)*

My Dad is Dead
by Amanda Hovseth

"Amanda…" my brother's voice breaks, like he's choking on something. "Amanda, wake up."

"What? Yah, Giles what…" I'm answering before my eyes open, my mind determined to respond before my body is willing.

"Dad's dead."

"Wow, really?" Wow? Did I really say wow? How did Giles get in here anyway? The door is open…I left the door open. When I went to bed a couple of hours ago I felt like I needed to. Twenty-six years old and still superstitious, ridiculous. Good. It would have hurt him to have come downstairs to a locked door.

"Yah." He coughs. "It just happened…just now."

"Okay, I'm coming." I reach for my glasses. Have to get upstairs. Can't wait for contacts, in a hurry…a hurry, why? Time is already up. Dead. Gone.

1

Permanent. I put on my glasses. My brother has left, he's waking up our other brother, right outside my room. My baby brother, the youngest, my babiest. Dad's dead. My room is dark but light shines through the opened doorway, I hurry towards it.

I am twenty-five years old, back in college, and looking forward to a road trip home with my dad for Thanksgiving Break. When he says he is proud of me now, it feels real because I am finally proud of myself. I had never really believed him before because a silent voice inside had always read the undertones in his words as disappointment. But, now my first book is published, and the majority of reviews are positive, his review is positive. He stops at every bookstore, school, and church on his road trips to tell them of my book. His ceaseless peddling of my work shown me he believes I have something worth saying.

He's temporarily stationed in Arkansas for the railroad and is going to drive out of his way to pick me up. We will have seven hours alone together and I am excited to talk to him about my new life, my new future.

My phone rings, he tells me he is running late. He took a nap after work and ended up sleeping much longer than anticipated. I say it's okay because I'll just nap while I wait for him.

Five minutes later he calls again. He sounds tired and he stumbles over his words. His boss says he has to work later that day. I might as well drive myself and we will meet back home. He is very sorry. We hang up and I stare at the phone. It's okay, I will still get to see him at home. But a realization penetrates my hopes, he has never missed family time for work before. He has always talked his way out of or into anything he wants. He is a real life con-artist. It doesn't compute. I shake my head and smile. He's an easily distracted guy, I'm sure it's nothing.

I use the bathroom and then grab my bag to leave. My phone rings. It's my mom, probably to check on our travel status. I answer. There's two seconds of silence…"Mom?" She sobs. I put my bags down, "What's wrong?"

"Have you left yet?"

"No, just about to."

"Good, you might need to go to Arkansas. Your father had a stroke, he's in the hospital. He says he's fine, but I know he's not. I'm sorry, you're the closest… he needs someone there."

"Okay…" I check google maps. "I can be there in eight hours." She thanks me. "I'll head out now." We hang up.

My phone rings. "Mandy?" My dad's voice is soft and wavers as if he is half asleep.

"I know, Dad, Mom just called me. I'm on my way to your hospital." I prepare for an argument. For him to say he's fine and my mom shouldn't have imposed…

"Are you sure?"

"Yes, I want to come."

3

"I'll text you my room number when they tell me."

"Love you, Dad, see you soon."

"Love you too."

I'm eighteen years old, my dad's calling me a stupid bitch and shoving me backwards. I fall onto the couch. My mother screams. "DON'T YOU EVER! Don't you ever talk to my daughter like that!" She runs at him and is pounding his chest and arms with her fists. He tries to block her blows while moving her away. She stops, exhausted and drops down next to me, pulling me into her arms. My dad is pressing his palms to his forehead. He throws a chair across the room. Then grabs car keys and heads out the front door. My mom is telling me not to listen to him. I barely hear her. I've never been called a bitch before, probably never will be again…at least not by someone who knows me.

I'm twenty-three years old, in a hotel in San Antonio. It's just me and my dad, he's been stationed here by the railroad, "borrowed out" they call it. He didn't want to go alone, so I decided to come with last minute. We've been here a month and a half now. He walks into the hotel room. I sit up in bed.

"Dad? Your back already? How'd you get back?" Normally I have to pick him up from the depot when his trains come in.

He's ruffling his hair; his eyes look hollow. He sits down to undo his work boots, but I can tell his skin is crawling. I wait, he'll talk, it's usually hard to stop him from talking.

"I hit a guy with my train. A boy. A man. He was in his twenty's." He glances at me every once in a while as he talks, but never makes eye contact. "He just stepped out in front of the train. I think he had headphones on. They phoned his parents...came to the tracks...apparently his brain wasn't right...he was...autistic or something."

"What? Why was he walking alone if he was autistic?"

"I know, right!" My dad is looking in the freezer, probably for ice cream. He pulls it out and puts it back, his skin is pale. "Some people just don't...they just don't think...I've hit cows before. Those trains they really leave nothing. Just pulp, barely tell it's human. He wasn't even close to the size of a cow." He's opening a bag of beef jerky.

"You know it's not your fault, right? You can't stop those trains on time. If you could have, you would have."

"Of course it's not my fault!" He paces back and forth across the length of the room. "No, I'm okay. I could see him there from a ways away. He was just walking, and I thought he would stop. I honked the horn just in case. He just kept walking. I thought for sure he would stop, why wouldn't he stop? Everyone stops. Then he didn't...he just didn't...stepped right out in front. Train didn't even bump. We pulled the breaks, I thought maybe he'd made it across, where I couldn't see. Trains take a long time to stop though."

"Are you fired?"

"I thought for sure I would be, but no. They want me to see a therapist and I have three days off of work. I told them I don't need a therapist, it wasn't my fault, I had no hand in it. His parents didn't even think so. Said he was living on his own for a year now, his roommate didn't know he was autistic." He takes a bite of his jerky. "Did you have plans for today?"

I do, I planned on meeting up with another railroader's wife and daughter and going to see the Madame Tussauds Wax Museum and Ripley's Believe It or Not. I ask if he wants to join.

He wrinkles his nose. "No, call me when you're done though."

"I can stay if you want."

"No, no Mandy, really I'm fine. It wasn't my fault." He's pacing again.

"Of course it wasn't but we can go another day, when you're at work."

"Really," He raises his voice and waves me off. "I'm fine. Call me after."

I leave the room and go to the museums. My phone is turned off inside because it's proper etiquette but when I make it to the gift shop and turn it on to call my father I realize I have six missed calls from him. My stomach flips and I call him back.

"Hello?" He answers and the phone crackles from wind blowing past. "Mandy? Where've you been?"

"In the museums I just got done and called you."

"It took that long?"

"Yah, I guess."

"Well I'm out front."

I turn to my friends and tell them where I'm going. As I walk to the front of the museum I spot him on a bench. He smiles and waves, but his eyes still look hollow. My heart aches. Poor guy, I should have never left him alone.

I'm nine years old and I've had a sleepless night. My parents are up, yelling at each other. I am lying in bed, pretending to be asleep and wondering if my sister in the bunk below me is actually asleep or if she is crying silently as well. I think that perhaps I should climb into bed with her and comfort her, but I don't know how. And if she is asleep then I'd only wake her up. So, we lie alone.

It's the next morning, I slip into the bathroom to use the toilet. My mom is in the shower but there is only one bathroom so we often double up.

She steps out as I'm brushing my teeth and I notice a long dark bruise on her right thigh. I ask if she's okay. She insists she is, she doesn't even know how she got that bruise.

My dad is nowhere to be seen. Someone has obviously tidied up the living room. Part of me is worried my dad won't come back. The other part knows that when I return from school there will be a new vase of flowers in the window and my parents will be waiting to hear how my day went. Like every time before.

I'm twenty-six years old, I came home for the summer because my dad has been diagnosed with cancer. Turns out he never had a stroke, only seizures brought on by brain tumors. My parents found me a job in road construction. I work anywhere from eight to fifteen hours a day. I'm walking up the stairs at five a.m. to get ready for work. My dad is awake in the living room. He always wakes up to send my brother and me off to work. He is looking at his phone. The low morning light allows the glow from his phone to accentuate his bone structure; sharp edges which used to be concealed in muscle. I wonder at how quickly his athletic physique has abandoned him.

"Mandy! Good morning! Have you seen these pictures of Giles and Jamus?"

Jamus is one of my cousins, he's four years old and can't digest any food at all, so he lives solely on a powdery nutrient substance. Quite frankly if people didn't know he was sick, they wouldn't guess it. He has curly red hair and chubby cheeks that even cherubs would envy. He enjoys labeling days as "Hug Day" and then distributing hugs throughout the house. When he has an allergic episode he dresses up as Iron Man and faces the situation head on. He is just absolutely adorable and ceaselessly cheerful. He also loves my father, calls him his best friend.

"Yah." I chuckle. "Jamus is super cute."

"I know!" My dad lets out what is best described as a girlish squeal. "I just keep thinking, he couldn't be any cuter, and then I flip to the next picture and...he is still even cuter!"

I laugh as I scoot my mom's cat out of the way and head out the front door.

His voice trails after, "I love you Mandy, and I'm proud of you."

He has said that every morning this summer.

I don't know who made it to the stairs first, me or my brothers. It doesn't matter, we have all climbed them and are now walking through the kitchen. My mom is already on the phone, it reminds me I'm late to the show. Time is slipping through my fingers at a speed I have never before encountered.

I'm twelve years old. My dad is standing by the stove with a big butcher knife in his hand. Neighborhood kids are watching and gasping as he continuously flips the knife into the air and catches it while making various faces of fear and shock. Tootsie Roll, our little Yorkshire Terrier, is hanging out by his feet. I call her over and pick her up. My dad glances my way and I frown at him. He knows this type of thing worries me. He calls out. "What, Mandy? You don't trust me?" Then he throws the knife even higher. I roll my eyes and leave the room. He can insist on dropping a knife on his foot, but he can't make me watch.

I am nineteen years old and I don't know how many days I have been lying in bed. I share a house with two friends. My dad hadn't wanted me to move out. He had yelled and yelled, calling me a fool for wasting the money. Then he had scoured my new apartment from top to bottom, looking for ways to make it safer. I don't know what I am doing with my life. College is boring, and the end seems so far away. I haven't picked a career and have no idea how to go about doing so. And I just keep gaining weight no matter how much I work out. A month ago some doctor gave me antidepressants and I don't know if I've left my bed since. I've missed every single college class, and I'll tell you what, I couldn't care less. I couldn't care if the world caught fire and burned up right in front of me. I couldn't care if a masked man entered my room and skinned a box of puppies. I couldn't care if Orlando Bloom asked me to dinner.

My phone rings. I answer. It's my father. I can barely hear him. I'm not sure if he's on speakerphone or if I'm still half asleep. While he talks I stare at the wall which I painted pink five months ago. The call is short. He tells me he loves me no matter what. He knows I'm going through some stuff and I might be worried he'd be disappointed. But he's not, it doesn't matter, he loves me anyway. The phone is beeping now. He must have hung up. I pull it away from my ear and notice the time. It's time to take my antidepressant. I pick up the box and roll onto my back. I hold the little white pods in front of my face and stare at them. The sun sets outside my window, slowly obscuring my view. I blink, throw the pods at the trash can, and stand up. It's time to take a shower.

I'm two years old, it's the middle of the night and my mom is pulling me out of bed and bundling me into the car. I ask her where we are going.

"To pick up your father."

It feels like we have driven forever. I am lying with my head resting by her pregnant belly when we pull up in front of a bar. I know it's a bar because of the neon lights. All bars have lights like that. She tells me to wait in the car and grabs a bat from the back seat. I wonder if my dad needs it to loan to a friend. Then she pauses and puts the bat back down.

Minutes later she is stomping out of the bar with my dad stumbling behind her, a bright red imprint of a palm on his cheek. They both get into the car without saying a word. I climb onto my dad's lap and I sleep the rest of the way home.

I turn the corner from the kitchen into the hallway. I know he will be there, at the end and to the right. I know he will. But he won't. I don't want to go. I have to go.

I'm twenty-four years old and at a Friday night Bible study with my father. People are asking him about his testimony. I smile because I know my dad doesn't like giving his testimony. He says that everyone thinks their life story is worth telling and most people are wrong. They insist. So, he gives them a piece of information which I always expected but never confirmed until then.

"When my lady told me she was pregnant with Mandy I panicked. I knew I should marry her and take care of the kid, but how was I supposed to do that? I was just a kid...I gambled a lot then, had gotten in too deep with the mafia. I started watching Oprah at my mom's house, thought it might help, it didn't much. My brother...the one, he's in Omaha now but was in Alliance, Denny, his wife got me an interview with Union Pacific Railroad. So, I drove through the night, from Chicago to Western Nebraska, took the test, and they gave me the job. I figured the mafia goons wouldn't drive to Nebraska lookin' for me, cuz really, you can't squeeze a dry sponge anyway. It worked, I paid them off later....But, if it wasn't for Lori's pregnancy I would have never looked to leave. If I had never moved to Nebraska I would have never met Pastor Rich. And if I had never met Rich, I...who knows for sure, but I think I would not have ever been convinced of my need for a Savior. I thought I was good enough to make God happy. I suppose everyone thinks that.

Ironic isn't it, wanting to earn love and failing; when all along I could've gotten it for free?"

I'm twenty-three years old. I just graduated from Bible College. My dad has called a family meeting. He wants to study the book of Proverbs. It's a good idea in theory, but family meetings never end well. This time it's my fault.

I'm mad. My stomach is clenching and my jaw is tightening. He's picked a study guide which is full of big words and non-sense phrases and ideas. I try to explain, "Proverbs is simple. This book is ridiculous. Man's way of overcomplicating God's Word to make ourselves seem more sophisticated." Normally my dad would understand this. I know for a fact he would agree with that general statement. But this isn't normally, this is a family meeting, and something goes wrong.

I'm grabbing my backpack, mentally calculating what is inside…my wallet, laptop, flash drive (with all my stories on it), phone…while I'm yelling at my dad and telling him I'd be better off alone. He yells back, something like, "Go ahead then!" I slam the door and stomp two miles to the library.

It's been five hours in the library. I have friends I can call, plenty of friends who would let me move in as long as I need. Even a couple of guys I know who would welcome the chance to get closer to me, guys my dad wouldn't approve of. But if I called them, if I called any of them, then the world would know. The world would hear of times he yelled, the time he broke our kitchen table, and they would see nothing else. They wouldn't actually see him and how much he truly has changed throughout the years. Everything he has worked for, everything I have worked for, would be ruined.

I'm walking through my parents' front door. The rest of my family is in the living room, quietly reading various books and watching TV. They look up when I come in, nod, and keep reading. My dad isn't there. I wonder if I can sneak into my room and pretend like nothing happened. Our cat, Shale, is walking by. He pauses in front of me. Shale was a rescue, so he's always hiding, never making a peep. Normally he runs when the front door is opened, instead he looks at me and walks down the hallway. I follow him. He leads me into my parents' room. My dad is on the bed with his back towards me and a phone in his hand. Shale jumps up onto the bed and meows. My dad turns around.

Instantly I start crying. And I say, "I came back. I don't want to break up our family over a dumb argument."

My dad is on his feet and hugging me. "I'm glad you came home. I didn't know where to look."

I'm twenty years old and I work as a secretary at Regional West Medical Center. My main job is organizing patients' charts and putting doctors' orders into the computer. It's been a hard twelve-hour shift and I'm exhausted when I walk through my parents' front door. A couple of my friends are over, so I try to put on a smile. My dad isn't fooled and instantly notices my sour mood. He insists on knowing what has upset me. I keep it simple because I want to move on, telling him the job is hard because I seldom get bathroom breaks and the doctors are pretty rude. He's furious. He calls my friend Andy over, grabs a phonebook and the car keys, and asks me what the doctors' names are.

I ask, "Why do you need their names?"

He says, "No one gets to be rude to my daughter, no matter who they are!"

Despite his rage, I smile. He and Andy plan on teaching the doctors "a lesson". I know what type of lessons my dad teaches people and I know our town needs its doctors, no matter how rude they are. So, I convince him the doctors weren't rude to me specifically. They are just rude in general. I really am okay. At this point, I'm beaming because of how protective my father and friends are, so he believes me and is content.

Instead of teaching lessons, he and Andy make homemade Chicago-style pizza.

I'm five years old. We are driving across the country, back home from my grandmother's funeral. It's nighttime. My parents laid down the seats in the back of our red minivan so that my siblings and I have a huge bed. I stare at the stars through the window and listen to the consistent calm of the wind blowing past.

My grandmother is dead. I cried when they told me, even though I barely knew her. I knew the concept of a grandmother, and mine was dead. Then I saw her body. It was white and cold, painted and posed. It was not her. They placed her body there, but she was not in it. I crawl to the front of the van and sit, leaning forward between my parents' seats. I want to know where grandma is.

They tell me something my mother has known since she was young, but my father had only learned recently. Grandma could be in Heaven if she had trusted God to get her there. They just don't know if she did.

I feel chills. How does someone trust God to get them to Heaven?

They tell me that every time we do the opposite of what God wants us to do, we have to be punished for it. If we decide to try to handle the punishment ourselves, then God can't let us go to Heaven, because not going to Heaven the punishment. But even when God is angry, He loves us and wants us to go to Heaven. So, He decided to take the punishment, Himself. He came to earth as Jesus, never did anything wrong, and then was killed in our place. Now we have a choice: we can pay for our sins ourselves, or we can believe that Jesus already paid for all of our sins and accept that payment as a free gift.

I told them I wanted Jesus to pay for my sins. They taught me how to pray. That night I met God. I have never felt more like I could fly than at that moment. I breathed deep. I told my sister about it and she joined me in prayer. Then I went to sleep, trusting my dad would get us home safely and knowing my God would someday bring our souls home safely.

I step into my parents' bedroom. It smells like a hospital: disgustingly sterile. My dad's body is there. His eyes are open. One is staring in a different direction than the other. His mouth is also wide open. It has been open for days. He slept with it open. My mom has turned off the oxygen machine and taken the breathing tubes out of his nose, he doesn't need them anymore. The machine's constant clicking and blowing was a reminder of how much it hurt him to breath—but now the world sounds wrong. We all step in, take a look, and leave. My mom is calling my uncles, they will be over soon. She says she has already called hospice. I say I am going downstairs to change since company will be coming.

I hurry back up the stairs. One of my brothers is telling the other that he needs to touch my father in order to make it real. The other is protesting, saying he doesn't need to. I brush by quickly and say, "Don't push him into anything, we all grieve different." Then I'm back in my parents' room, alone with my father. I step up to him and place three fingers under his jawbone as if to take a pulse…I'm six years old, I've had a nightmare. I know if I wake my father up he will let me climb into bed and I'll be safe. I can sleep easy…No. No. I'm twenty-six years old. I'm twenty-six years old and I'm touching his neck. His skin isn't quite cold yet. He's not waking up. He's not moving. He's dead. My dad is dead.

I say, "I love you Dad. I'll see you later."

I'm twenty-five years old, it's Thanksgiving Break and I've made it to the hospital in Arkansas. My dad is in the hospital bed. He's on the phone with our pastor. I hear him struggle to speak so I step into the bathroom to give him privacy. It's on speakerphone so I can still hear. My dad is always worried cell phones will give us cancer, so he doesn't like holding them up to his head. Our pastor doesn't want to let my dad give up hope. He says, "There's still a chance. You could survive…you're not dying before me." I stare at the sink because I don't want to look in the mirror. My dad says, "No listen. You know the story of John Bradford, right? I want my kids to know. I want, after all this, the one thing they should learn from my life…'There but for the grace of God go I'."

I take my fingers off of my dad's neck. I walk out of his bedroom and into the bathroom. I close the door, and I cry.

"I'm the big person, you're the little person; little people do what big people tell them to do."

-     *Dan Hovseth (when arguing with his children)*

Sunlight
by Amanda Hovseth

"What if it doesn't work? What if she gets sick?"

"We'll take it slow. The sun is setting, even if the treatment doesn't work she is in very little danger and if there are any warning signs then we will draw back."

Their voices are in the background, I can't focus on them now, there's just too much going on. Instead I stare at the cover of my favorite childhood book. It's about a baby duck looking for his mother. I've always known who my mother was. She's the one who's scared I'll be dead in the next couple of minutes.

"All of the trial runs have been successful. Not a single patient has had any complications so far."

"So far! So far, is not comforting! My Nadine is too precious to risk on your uncertainties!"

I flip through the pages, watching the little duck travel around the world, meeting new and unfamiliar creatures. I was born with an extreme photosensitivity, I've never had the luxury of getting lost.

"And what about her eyes! Her skin might be fine but her eyes have never even been exposed to florescent lights!"

"Mother," I say gently. I close my book and stand up. "That's what these sunglasses are for. I'm eighteen now and you promised it was my decision."

Tears sprout from my mother's eyes as she steps over and puts a hand on each cheek. "My dear girl. You have everything you could possibly want. Why are you doing this to me?"

I take one of her hands into mine. "I'm not doing this to you, I'm doing it for me." Then I turn to Doctor Hinkley. "Let's get started." I place the sunglasses on my face, instantly turning the dimly lit room to a vast array of shadows.

My mother sobs as the Doctor takes my hand and leads me to the window. I stand in front of the thick, heavy curtain. He grabs a corner, causing a puff of dust to abandon its resting place. I sneeze, then the curtain is gone, and I forget to breath.

Dust is still floating in the air, only now I can see it. I wave my hand through it and watch as the light quickly swirls around my motions, only to slow down, as if stuck in molasses, the second my hand retreats. A bird flutters past the window causing my eyes to snap from the show in front of my nose to the world beyond. I gasp and step forward, planting my palms on the chilled glass. A large orange dome is sitting on the horizon, the air around it flows in waves of yellow, red, and pink.

"Is that…?"

"That's the sun." My mother is at my side now. She slides an arm around my waist. My eyes traverse the wheat fields. Every once and awhile a breeze causes the stalks to sway. They appear to be playing with the sun and their laughter shines gold. I laugh along with them.

"How are you feeling dear?" My mother holds me tighter but my mind is rolling in the supple, emerald grass of my front yard and holding the smiling lady bug which just landed on the outside of the window frame.

My mother insists on an answer. Somewhere far away my voice replies.

"Alive. I'm actually alive."

"If you don't learn to laugh at yourself, you'll be the only one in the room not laughing."

-     *Dan Hovseth (learned from his father Larry)*

Yorkshire Blues

by Amanda Hovseth

Francine sat at the airport food court on a hard, grey chair, trying to keep her camera from touching the sticky table-top. A man sat at the table next to her, picking at a plate of Chinese food. A couple yards behind the man, William sauntered back and forth, holding a plastic tray. He glanced at Francine, winked, and then threw himself to the ground, swinging the tray against the floor as hard as he could. The man jumped and turned his head toward the noise. While he was turned, Francine quickly reached out to snatch a handful of saucy breaded chicken.

"Hey! What are you doing?" The man exclaimed.

Francine gasped and looked up, still holding the dripping meat in an outstretched fist. "Nothing." She said as she stood and shoved the slimy mess into her pants pocket.

The man furrowed his brow. "What the—"

"We're on a mission!" Will yelled as he jumped around the man, grabbed Francine's elbow, and pulled her away. "Fortune favors the fast!" He hollered over his shoulder.

"That's not how the saying—" The man called back but his voice trailed off as the pair of ten-year-olds rounded a corner.

They sprinted across the concourse to the baggage claim area, where they both flopped into chairs, gasping for air between laughs.

"Okay, okay." Will raised both hands, palms out. "It's time for phase two: confirm mission objective." He turned slightly to his left and motioned with his eyes toward a high-heeled blond sitting a few rows down. On a chair to her right, sat her purse. Sticking out of the top of the purse was the poofy brown head of a miniature Yorkshire Terrier.

Francine nodded and pulled the cap off her camera lens. She zoomed in on the dog and snapped a couple pictures. Then the two leaned in together and stared down at the photos on her screen.

Will nodded. "Mission objective confirmed. Doggo is still sad, operation 'Cheer Up Sad Doggo' is a go."

Francine snorted and examined the picture closer. "How can you even tell he's sad?"

"He's wearing a blue bowtie, of course he's sad," Will insisted. "Besides, he's stuck waiting at an airport, just like us."

"Oh, goodness," Francine chastised. "My mom will be here to pick us up soon enough. Seems someone who gets to go on a fun summer trip to New York with his bestie should grumble less."

"Yeah, Yeah." Will flicked his hand in her direction. "You're right, but you're losing focus on our mission. When do you think was the last time this poor sad doggo got to taste meat?"

Francine leaned forward, eyeing the dog. "Probs never. His person looks fancy. I'm sure she only feeds him fancy things like…egg pies."

"Egg pies?" Will wrinkled his nose and chuckled. "Do you mean quiche?"

"Sure, whatever." She rolled her eyes. "Fancy it up why don't you, Mr. Fancy Pants."

"At least I'm not Miss Saucy Pants."

The pair made eye contact and broke into giggles.

After a few seconds, Will straightened up. "Phase three is set to commence."

Will slinked out of his chair, cleared his throat, and nodded at Francine. She handed him her camera while nodding back; and he shot her a close-lipped smile before turning toward the blond lady.

"Excuse me ma'am," he said as he stepped up to the lady's left side. "I couldn't help but notice you are the prettiest lady in this joint. Any chance you'd let me take a picture of you?"

The lady furrowed her brow and eyed Will up and down. "How old are you?"

"Ten whole years ma'am," he answered.

The lady sniffed and hesitantly turned toward him. "I suppose there's no harm in a photo… so long as you stop calling me ma'am," she added with a half-smile.

"Okay, thank you so much!" Will said as he jumped up and down and slowly began removing the cover from the camera lens.

Meanwhile, Francine slid into the chair next to the dog and held a piece of chicken in front of it's face. The dog's nose wiggled at the meat, but then he whined and ducked further into the bag.

What? She thought to herself. *What's the matter?* She peeked into the purse and whispered to the shiny brown eyes blinking up at her, "It's just meat. You'll love it, I promise." She stuck her hand into the bag and held the meat in front of the dog's face again, while glancing at Will.

"So, why is a lady like you sitting around in a baggage claim area?" He was asking while snapping pictures.

"I'm waiting for my driver, he's stuck in traffic," the lady answered as she moved from pose to pose. Then her phone began ringing in one of the purse's outside pockets.

Francine quickly dropped the meat next to the dog and jumped out of her seat. She was already in the next aisle by the time the lady tore herself away from the camera to grab her phone.

Moments later, Will stepped up to Francine's side. "Hey, isn't that your mom?"

"Where?" Francine turned in a full circle before spotting her mom waving as she walked through one of the doorways. "Oh, Yeah!" Francine waved back. "Let's go!"

They snatched up their luggage and made their way to the exit.

"Did we succeed?" Will asked as they walked.

"I don't know." Francine frowned. "He wouldn't eat it from my hand, but I left him some in the purse."

"Hmmm…" Will responded.

"Francie! And this must be William!" Francine's mom exclaimed as she pulled them both into a hug.

While the pair stared out from each side of the hug, the blond lady walked by with her purse slung over her shoulder. As she passed, the little dog's head popped out of the bag.

Francine and William gasped in unison as they noticed him excitedly lick at the sticky, saucy fur all around his mouth.

"I want to fly and shoot fire out of my butt, but we don't always get what we want."

- *Dan Hovseth*

Climate Changes
by Amanda Hovseth

Eliza stood in front of their train car window watching white flakes descend upon the world—a sight the heat of her southern hometown had never let her see. She bounced up and down as she imagined opening the window and leaping into a mass of powdered sugar. It would billow up around her as she landed gently in its sweet embrace. Then it would quickly morph from light and airy to smooth and creamy. She would take it in her hands and mold it gently into delicate little flowers—like the kind she had seen on Aunt Alice's wedding cake—then pop them into her mouth one by one as an endless supply flowed freely from the clouds. She pressed her nose against the glass and breathed deep, before leaning back. Her perfect crimson curls swayed to and fro with the motion of the train.

Her father slid over. She was standing where his legs were meant to be so he lifted them up and laid them across the seat next to him. With his back to the window he smiled at her then turned his head and breathed out long and hard against the glass. Eliza's jaw dropped as she watched the haze spread. Then her father reached out with his finger and drew a lopsided heart right in the middle.

"For you darling." He reached over and pulled one of her curls straight to watch it bounce quickly back into place.

She giggled and leaned forward to mimic his breath on the window, just as her mother re-entered their cabin.

"Goodness! Did you teach her that? You'll leave all sorts of smudges on that glass," Her mother scolded.

Eliza's father just grinned and winked at his daughter as he placed his wide brimmed cowboy hat on his head.

"Mama, when the train stops I'm going to run and jump into the snow!"

"You'll do no such thing." Her mother pulled her over and began adding layers to her outfit. First slipping on gloves which made her hands look like fat little penguin flippers, and then stuffing them down through sleeves on a coat which, when zipped up, forced her arms to stick out at angles.

"But, mother…" Eliza said as her mouth watered at the thought of burying her face in a giant snow drift and licking away at its smooth crystals.

"No buts!" She waggled a finger in Eliza's face while plastering her curls flat against her head under a stocking cap with ear flaps. Then she added, while wrapping a long scarf around her neck, making certain to loosely cover her nose and mouth. "I know it looks exciting, but snow is bitter cold and I won't have you catching your death over some childish fancy."

Eliza's arms struggled against her prison as she attempted to cross them and caused a puff of air to squeeze out from the lining. She turned towards her father. He smiled softly at the sight of her narrowed eyes and furrowed brow—barely visible between the warm fabrics—but then he simply shrugged while zipping up his own coat.

Her protest was interrupted by the loud screech of the train's brakes. Once it came to a complete stop, her father swung her up into his arms and carried her into a winter wonderland.

Eliza's eyes blinked quickly as she peered out over her father's shoulder, scanning the expanse of white. Snowflakes landed on her eyelashes and clung to the ends of her hair. Despite herself, she smiled. Her mind wandered to an ice cream cone she had devoured two days ago and she imagined a vanilla so delicious she would never crave a different flavor ever again. She stuck out her tongue eagerly, but all she tasted was laundry detergent as the wool of her scarf brushed roughly against it.

"Stop having fun with people who aren't here."

- Dan Hovseth (to people on cellphones)

Friend Zone
by Amanda Hovseth

"You've been really social lately. Why can't you just only be social with me, like you normally are?"

Janene's voice rang in Adam's head, milky smooth with a teasing wine, as he watched the other girl sitting across from him. Her lips were full and slightly pink, always tilting up in the corners. Janene's usually tilted down but every once and awhile, if he was truly clever, he could get her to offer up a smirk.

"Do you wear lipstick?" Adam asked before taking a bite out of his turkey sandwich.

Emily was drinking her sweet tea and kept her mouth on the straw as she wrinkled her nose at him. He watched the brown shadow of the liquid retreat back down the straw. Janene only drank unsweetened tea.

"What? No." She answered while setting the cup down. "That straw would be a straight up mess if I was." Then she narrowed her eyes at him in mock suspicion. "Why do you ask?"

"No reason."

She raised her eyebrows and took a bite from a glossy red apple.

"I have a friend who usually uses that color of lipstick." He said.

"Apple color?"

"It's called *crimson sunset*."

"Sounds dazzling."

"You should meet her. We've been friends longer than I can remember. I think the two of you would really hit it off."

"Sure, what's she like?"

"Well she's…you know how you like to…" His eyes traced the ceiling tiles. "I don't know, I means she's just Janene. Here I'll show you a picture." He pulled his phone from his pocket and quickly swiped to a photo of him and Janene making fish faces.

"Cute," Emily smiled gently and handed the phone back to him. "So, are you guys…I mean have you guys been more than friends?"

Adam's face turned bright red. He cleared his throat and stared at the table while shoving his phone back into his pocket.

"Okay, no big deal." Emily tossed a potato chip onto his plate. "Here have one on me."

He glanced up at her. She was drinking her tea again and leaning back in her chair, watching his every move. He sniffed and scratched the side of his nose. Then his phone chirped.

"It's Janene, she wants to go get ice cream. Wanna come?"

"Can't sorry, I have class in thirty. You can go though."

Adam chewed his bottom lip. "Well I don't know if I want any." He set the phone on the table but left the screen on. "What class is it?"

"Logic and Critical Thinking."

"Oh good, maybe once you can think critically you'll finally see that Batman is much sexier than Captain America."

Emily's laugh filled the room like chiming cymbals and when she made eye contact with Adam she spread her lips into a wide smile that was so bright he could have sworn he heard it *ting*. Then her laugh settled into soft giggles and each one of them made his chest feel like it was filling with bubbles and about to burst. He grinned and ate the potato chip as his phone screen faded to black.

"Always practice defensive driving; you can have the right of way and still end up dead."

-    *Dan Hovseth*

Informed Consent
by Amanda Hovseth

When I answer the phone I don't realize it will change my identity.

Before I say "hello"— I am just another girl in a hotel room, the burn of cheap whisky in my throat, the air filled with cigarette smoke blowing from the lungs of the stranger sitting across from me.

Before I say "hello"— he says he wants whatever I want; a one-night stand, a summer fling, a marriage, whatever I want. I don't know what I want yet, so no one decides and we spend the night acting on impulse, pretending skin on skin contact will provide an epiphany.

Before I say "hello"— he is telling me about his life. I am impressed by his honesty and openness. We have a lot in common; maybe we could make this work. Sure, he has four children with two different women, but he says he's not with either of them anymore, just visits his kids. I remind myself that it's the same with most guys my age.

Before I say "hello"— we have intimate relations six times. I learn he's afraid of teeth and isn't a big fan of hands. I learn he's tough on the streets, a bullet hole in his upper thigh to prove it.

Before I say "hello"— the sun peeks through the curtains and I groan at the alarm clock. He laughs, pulls me in close, and kisses my shoulder.

After I say "hello"— I realize this was the only time he kissed me, once, on my shoulder, with the birds chirping the start of a new day, a new beginning.

Before I say "hello"— he gets upset because I let another guy drive my van. I roll my eyes but am careful to not do it again.

Before I say "hello"— our time together in the same town is running short. I convince myself it doesn't matter. I'll enjoy it while it lasts.

Before I say "hello"— we talk about the possibility of meeting again someday. Maybe the timing will be better. Either way we will keep in touch, look out for each other.

When I say "hello"— I listen as my friend tells me her discovery, the results of a few clicks on Facebook. I feel my old identity slipping away, like a mask I had forgotten I was wearing.

"I guess this makes me the other woman," I say.

"You think it's the physical body that you're attracted to, but it's not. You're attracted to what it's attached to: a soul and its personality. Otherwise, you'd be fine with a pair of boobs on a plate, not attached to anything."

- *Dan Hovseth (advice to Junior High boys)*

She Won't Let Go
by Giles Hovseth

Sam had heard about her long before he saw her. She was desperate. She was dirty. She was deadly.

Sam had made up his mind about her long before he saw her. Delilah was disgusting, and he would despise her at all costs.

Nobody had told Sam that she was desirable.

He took a wrong turn walking home. He knew the street would take him near her, but he thought he would be safe. He expected a wretch, until he saw Delilah for the first time.

She danced high above him, waving at passersby from the platform of a billboard which sold good times and fast money. Her laughter trailed through the air, enchanting and alluring. Sam only looked for a moment, but in that moment her flowing hair and shapely body made an indelible impression, urging him to stare.

He quickly averted his eyes. This must have been her. He never should have looked.

She was gorgeous, but how was that possible?

Sam stared at the ground and sped his way down the street. He tried to settle back into his old ways, despising her from years of hearing derogatory remarks at her expense, but long after he left, her laughter echoed in his mind.

Sam spent a week avoiding the street. He went about his business, but with each passing moment of boredom his mind would find its way back to the billboard and the woman who danced before it. He knew it would be wrong to see more of her, but he could not rest knowing she was still there.

The chaos in his brain churned and ached until it spewed forth a compromise: he would go to see the billboard. Delilah was insignificant. What mattered to him now were the words on the billboard. He had to know what they said, and if he chanced upon Delilah, he would simply walk away. That's what Sam had told himself.

As he neared the street, a faint and lilting melody drifted into his ears:

> I've come outside to see your face,
> I searched for hours in every place.
> My bed is soft and silky smooth,
> It's time now to lay down and move.

Let's drink deep of love till morning.
Enjoy ourselves in love, enjoy ourselves in
love.

The soothing song quickened Sam's pulse, and his feet brought him to stand beneath the billboard. He gazed upwards to see the advertisement's words proudly proclaim, "Stolen water is sweet, food eaten in secret is delicious!" He could not see Delilah.

Stunned at her unexpected absence, Sam looked up and down the street. He jumped at the sight of a large man walking towards him. The man's eyes were sunken and desperate. His beard was unkempt and overgrown. The man gave off an air of loneliness unlike anything Sam had experienced before.

The man walked past Sam without a glance, and Sam's heart sank. His stomach turned and tears sprung to his eyes. He could not shake the feeling that he had done something wrong. The guilt was overwhelming. He slowly lowered himself to the ground. *Where am I*, he thought. *Where am I.*

He felt a light touch on his shoulder. Warm breath blew past his cheek. A soft and enticing female voice lulled out, "I've been looking for you."

Sam turned his head to find the most beautiful woman he had ever seen, the first *woman* he had ever seen, kneeling down beside him. Her shapely breasts rose and fell beneath a thin white blouse, moving to the pleasing rhythm of her breath. Her hair flowed elegantly around her shoulders, plush and comforting. Her lips and cheeks seemed supple and delicate, welcoming a gentle kiss or a smooth caress. Her face glowed in the sun, and her eyes belied an aching thirst.

Sam felt a new longing stir inside of him. He wanted to hold her. He wanted to kiss her. He wanted to be swallowed up inside of her, engulfed in her essence, and he wanted to consume her until he burst in glorious communion with the woman of his dreams. He now had an appetite only she could sate. He wanted to claim her.

His surge of desire stunned Sam with its suddenness. In his silence, Delilah spoke again, "I've been looking for you."

"For me?" asked Sam.

Delilah giggled. "I love simple men, like you."

"I'm hardly a man."

"You're man enough for me," Delilah said, lightly squeezing Sam's shoulder.

Sam's heart raced, accepted. "Can...can I kiss you?"

Delilah smiled, then leaned in with puckered lips. *So close,* thought Sam, *She's so close.* He breathed in to savor the moment...but something smelled...wrong. In his hesitation, Delilah pulled Sam to her lips.

Their connection was electric. Energy pulsed through Sam's body like never before. He had made a connection to something he could hardly have imagined only weeks ago. He had made a connection to Delilah.

Blood rushing through his body, Sam wrapped his arms around her and pushed his chest to hers. His lungs expanded, pulling her lips further into him, bringing her musk to the forefront of his subconscious: enticing, intoxicating, deadly.

Delilah pulled back from Sam, his face burning red, a small drop of scarlet resting on the left commissure of her lips. Her tongue moved sensually around her wicked smile. "Come with me. My bed is ready, and we can enjoy ourselves until morning."

She stood, and Sam followed. She walked, and Sam followed. He stared at the shifting curves of her buttocks, squeezing against the tight denim which was lucky enough to embrace her body. Without thinking, he reached forward and cupped her left cheek in his right hand. She smiled back at him and opened the door to a beaten and run-down house.

They stepped past the threshold to look upon a darkened stairway descending into the ground. Sam closed the door behind them and followed Delilah down the stairs. Light blue candles lit their way, casting a strange glow on the walls, causing Delilah's beauty to become more opulent with each step they took. Another doorway stood at the bottom of the stairs, but this door, made of ancient oak, was already open.

They entered the new room, and the door shut itself behind them. A large and luxurious bed seemed to float in an abyss of nothingness. Sam saw only Delilah as she strode to the bed, climbed to the center, and slowly worked her shirt over her head, tantalizingly revealing her two perfect breasts, too perfect for Sam to handle.

Sam tore his own clothes from his flesh and rushed to the bed. She laughed as he wrapped his arms around her waist and buried his face in her chest, rubbing his manhood against her jeans. "Do it," She said. "Drink deep of my love."

He pulled her jeans from her legs, exposing her most delightful part. Sam fell inside, engulfed in the glory of the moment, swallowed up by the sensation of a newfound sexuality more pleasing than anything he had known before. Her moans filled his ears, her scent filled his nostrils, and the euphoria of his thrusts filled his waking mind. Delilah was his delight, and she made him blossom, then bloom, exploding into a satisfaction and contentment that put Sam's heart at ease as he rolled off of her sweat-drenched body.

He closed his eyes to revel in the moment, but the sexual haze started to fade away. Breathing deep, he smelled her musk again. He knew now what was wrong. She smelled sour. Sam breathed in again and realized *he* smelled sour too.

This sudden shift shocked Sam, and a wave of displeasure started to take hold. He felt strange. He felt as if something was missing. In all the fun and joy Delilah had brought him, there had been some unspoken promise left unfulfilled, some deep-seated desire left unmet. His chest felt empty.

Sam opened his eyes and looked at his own naked body. Immediately, he saw a glaring absence, a gaping hole right where his heart should have been.

"No!" He screamed. Dread began to overwhelm his senses. Tears poured from his now sunken eyes. "No!"

Sam curled up in horror, shaking from the pain. He lay in darkness, weeping and sobbing until his cries were outdone. Delilah's moans echoed in the room once again.

Sam uncurled and looked across the bed. A faceless man rammed himself into Delilah, over and over, as Delilah rubbed her breasts against the man's chest and gasped from the man's indomitable passion, their love-making occurring in a wide-spread puddle of Sam's blood.

"No..." Sam cried again. "Please stop."

Delilah did not stop.

Sam crawled off the bed, shaking in sorrow. He reached his clothes, opened the ancient door, and glanced back at his love enjoying another man on the ruins of his former self.

Sam closed the door and climbed the stairs, straining against the exhaustion that lethargized his normally lithe muscles. He reached the exit and opened the door to the blinding light of the outside world. The light revealed that he was naked, his missing heart exposed to reality. To cover up his shame, Sam pulled his clothes on faster than he ever had before. He walked back to the street, where he saw a teenage boy staring up at the billboard. As he approached the boy, Sam heard the boy read to himself aloud, "Stolen water is sweet, food eaten is secret is delicious."

Sam tried to shuffle by the boy, but he was too tired to walk silently. The boy turned and jumped at the sight of Sam, his eyes going wide. The boy asked, "Hey dude, is everything okay?"

Sam avoided making eye contact and said, "Yeah. Everything... everything's fine."

"Oh, okay," said the boy. "Hey, have you seen a girl named Delilah around here? All the guys in my class say she's really cool."

Vomit launched from Sam's mouth and landed on the boy's shoes. The boy didn't seem to notice, so Sam said, "No, I haven't seen her. Never seen her before."

The boy raised an eyebrow, skeptical, but said, "Oh, alright. Have a nice day."

The boy walked away, and Sam puked again at the thought of this boy with Delilah. It was wrong. It was all wrong. Shaken by disgust, Sam returned home and went to sleep.

For the next few months, Sam dreamt of Delilah. His loneliness would succumb to desire, and he'd return to her time and time again for the fleeting pleasure of her distant company. He grew to resent himself for his dependency on her pseudo-love, and he tried to resent her, but he always returned. His emptiness became a part of his life, and he learned well how to cover up the absence of his heart when around family and friends. They could never know that he had seen Delilah. They would never understand his emptiness, and he could never be free of it.

There were some men he grew envious of. These men had been with Delilah, and they knew no shame from their dalliances with her. They went around without shirts, examining the holes Delilah had left in each other's chests. She had taken one with a knife, another with a sword, and still another with a sharpened dildo the man had requested specifically. They boasted of anal beads, fisting, and bukakke, and Sam was disgusted by their boldness but wondered at their freedom. Sam could know no such freedom. They boasted of pleasures Delilah had brought them, but Delilah had brought Sam no true pleasures, only empty sex.

After one particularly horrific night with Delilah and their sexual escalation, Sam left her dwelling an emotional wreck. Engorged with self-loathing and despair, Sam could handle his loneliness no longer. He had to tell somebody about his affair. He had to let somebody know.

His emotional hurricane brought Sam, drenched in tears, to the doorstep of his father's house. Sam steeled his reserve and rang the doorbell. Sam's father answered, eyes widening at the sight of his own son in crisis. Before his father could speak, Sam sputtered out, "Dad, I'm in so much pain. I've seen Delilah. I know you told me not to, but I saw her. It hurts so much, I can't take it any longer."

Sam crumpled to the ground, shaking in pain. His father sighed and lowered himself to the ground next to Sam. His father said, "It's okay son. You don't have to take it anymore. You can get free of her."

"No I can't," cried Sam, "it's impossible."

"Son. Look at me."

Sam turned his head to look at his father. His father had raised his shirt, baring his chest to the world. A living heart beat in his chest, connected to his body through years of scar tissue and regrowth. He had seen Delilah too, and he had broken free.

Despair turned to awe, as Sam saw his father in a whole new light. Sam knew that his father understood, and Sam knew that he could get his heart back too.

The next day, Sam returned to the street where Delilah lived. She was on the billboard once again, dancing like in the days of old. As he approached her house, he could hear her sing, *"Enjoy ourselves in love, enjoy ourselves in love."*

There is no love here, thought Sam. He entered her home, seeing the despondency in which she lived. Creaking boards, rotting posts, rusting hinges, sputtering flames, all apparent to his wizened eyes. He reached the bottom to find the ancient door wide open, as it always was.

The abyss welcomed him as an old friend, supporting his weight as he strolled to the bed he'd lain in a hundred times before. He grabbed the blankets and tossed them to the side. He reached below the mattress and pulled on the sheets. They stuck to the mattress with ages of congealed sweat and semen, Sam removed them from the bed to the sound of a sickening slick.

The mattress, once comfortable and luxurious, revealed itself to be lumpy and dingy, its excessive use exposed in the light. Sam drew a knife from his pocket, and slashed at the fabric of the mattress. Between the cloth and the springs, Sam saw hundreds of dry and dusty hearts, flimsy from years of disuse.

Sam slit the palm of his left hand and let his blood drip onto the hearts. From deep inside the pile, he heard the dull thrum of a heart beating to a rediscovered tune. He dug through the pile and found his heart, frail and broken, but willing to work again. He lifted his shirt and placed his heart back in his chest, small strands of flesh jumping to reconnect the heart to the body. Footsteps sounded behind him, and Sam turned around.

Delilah entered the room leading a teenage boy with his hand on her buttocks. As if Sam were invisible, she led the boy past him and to the torn open bed, laying down on top of it, with the boy moving to get inside her.

"I'm leaving you," Sam said, face hardened with resolve. "You will never see me again."

In between moans and pants, Delilah replied, "Do you think I care?"

Sam thought for a moment, then said, "No. No I don't think you do."

He turned to the ancient door, still open for him to leave, and Delilah called out once more, "I'll see you again. I know I will."

Sam stopped. "Maybe," pointing to his heart he said, "but you will never see this again."

As Sam left the room, he thought he heard her moans come a little less often, and he had the strange feeling that he had won.

When he left the house, he saw a pre-teen boy staring at the billboard.

Sam walked up to the boy, who turned and jumped at Sam's arrival.

"Hey mister, is everything okay?" asked the boy.

"No," said Sam. "This billboard called to me once, like it is to you now. It calls to those who lack judgement saying, 'stolen water is sweet; food eaten in secret is delicious!' But they don't know that the dead are there. Her guests are in the depths of the grave. I was one of them."

Without a word, the boy turned and left the street. Sam walked the other way, free from her grip for the first time in years.

"You're too young for a relationship. Guys your age have nothing to offer yet: no house, no career, no money. Why would you be attracted to someone who can't provide for you? Don't waste your time, wait until you're older."

- Dan Hovseth (on high school relationships)

An Iron Love
by Amanda Hovseth

She gripped the knotted roots in front of her, there had to be a way out. To think, a lumberjack's daughter was unable to escape a cage made of wood.

Her father's image played across the back of her eyelids. His sun-crisped skin, even redder when enraged. His thick, all-encompassing beard—long and gray streaked—trembling with his bottom lip. The rifle in his hand, its stock pressed against the floor as his knuckles whitened.

"You do not understand love!" She had yelled at him with tears streaming down her face. "There is nothing more important!" She had slammed the front door without looking back, intent on meeting the boy she loved at their usual tree encircled destination.

She would give anything for her father to be here now. To smell the sticky pine sap on his plaid shirt as he would pull her into a hug with his arms that were hardened from a life of labor. To hear the gentle rumble of his laughter and see his yellowed teeth shine. Yes, she would give anything, anything at all just so she could say she was sorry.

A cool breeze played about her legs pulling up the pleats of her blood red dress. She didn't bother pushing them down, instead she clutched her arms to her chest in a shiver. Sleeveless with a sweet-heart cut had been a good choice out in the sun, but, here, deep in the darkest brambles of the woods, there was no warmth to be found. Her fingers fiddled with the chain around her neck. Pure iron, it was heavy and always gave her skin a greenish rash, but it had been her mother's and was all she had left of her, so she had worn it today. Today, the day when all her romantic dreams were supposed to have come true.

The bushes to her right began to creak and shudder as they untangled themselves and shimmered apart to make a path. Lily pressed herself against the side of her cage which was furthest away from the path as a mixture of masculine and feminine laughter echoed toward her.

"Oh Foster, imagine the party Mab will throw in your honor when you bring her this little treat." A female voice chimed through the gap as their forms began to appear. "The Winter Court will have a riot celebrating such a valuable hostage! Ah, and the marvelous battles to ensue once Oberon finds out—" She trailed off in a high-pitched squeal while clenching her fists to her chest.

"I know darling, I couldn't believe my fortune." He responded while lifting her into the air and spinning her in a circle.

Tears sprang up in Lily's eyes as she took in his strange form. His skin had turned an iridescent blue and his eyes were now golden, but there was no mistaking him. She had fallen in love with every move of his body. The way his long, silver hair played with the breeze and his smile only turned up on the right side of his mouth. The first time she had seen him had been during one of her walks in the forest. He had glided up to her like smooth ice, with inhuman ease. She covered her mouth with her hand as a sob caught in her throat. Inhuman, she should have seen. He was too perfect. It was all too perfect.

"Who...what are you?" She choked out.

In a matter of seconds, the female was at her cage. Her clawed fingers spidered around the wooden bars and her grin of blinding white razors pressed against a gap. "I think the correct question is, what are *you*?" Her voice was like the chiming of icicles being blown together as she reached out with one long diamond claw and scratched a small incision into Lily's right arm. A drop of blood oozed onto the tip of her nail. Snarling, she brought it to her mouth and licked it off. Her golden eyes narrowed for a second as she pondered the metallic taste, then a grin spread—wider than her heart-shaped face should have allowed—and she glided over to Foster, pulling him into a full ten-second kiss. When he came up for air his eyes met Lily's and a feral snarl appeared on his face.

"Lily, oh my dear little Lily pad," his voice was like smooth butter as he walked closer to her. "Love is a funny thing now isn't it? Makes people do funny things." He reached through the cage and brushed a strand of her hair out of her eyes. She flinched at his touch and swiped his hand away. He laughed. "To late for that darling. Oh, don't be so upset, I do love you of course. I love you for what you are going to bring me. At first I thought you would just be a fun little game but the more time I spent with you, the more I realized your potential. Who you really are. Not just a boring human are you?"

"What are you talking about?" She crossed her arms.

"Tell me, what did your mother die of?" he asked.

Lily furrowed her brow and clenched her arms tighter.

He laughed and rolled his eyes. "Nothing? You give me nothing? Well fair enough, I suppose you've already given plenty. But think of this, when you walk in the forest how do you feel? Unusually comfortable? Like you can breathe easier? Do you dream of flying through sparkling skies and dancing in wild gardens? Do you really know who your father is?"

"Just shut up already, of course I know who my father is." She said as her bottom lip quivered.

"Very well, it's time we were on our way anyway." He stepped back from the cage and with a snap of his fingers the bars parted. "Come along then." He motioned with his hand and a branch nudged her forward. Her legs trembled as she stepped out of the cage. One of her red heels snagged on a stray root, causing her to sprawl forward onto the ground.

Foster's girlfriend groaned, so he chuckled and mockingly chastised her, "Now, now, Nixie give little Lily a break. I'm sure it's hard for her with all that human DNA polluting her royal blood." He reached down and patted Lily on the back, but a second later he hissed and flinched away as a sizzling sound came from a spot he had touched on her neck.

"What is that?" He accused pointing at her mother's chain as he pressed his other, injured hand to his chest. "Get rid of it!" he commanded.

Lily slowly stood up, gripping the chain around her neck, eyeing him with clenched jaw. "No, it was my mother's."

"Your mother's, of course." He resumed composure, sliding his fingers through his hair. "Well it can't come where we are going so you better take it off and leave it here."

It was Lily's turn to laugh. "Why would I ever do that?"

Foster ground his teeth and clenched his hands. Then his hair began to float around him as the breeze gathered into a strong wind.

Lily gasped as the wind began pushing her towards him.

His voice grew deep as thunder as he said, "It is iron, and iron is poison to our land. Surely it can't be good for you either. Now stop being stubborn and—"

Nixie interrupted, "Come on Foster, just grab her," she yelled above the roaring wind. "We don't have time for games. We have to get her to the Winter Court before they notice she's not at home and Oberon sends—"

Just then a raven burst through the trees and swooped down to claw at Foster's face.

"No!" Nixie had time to scream before hundreds of more ravens swarmed in from the sky, engulfing the couple in a flurry of beaks and feathers.

The wind abandoned its tugging on Lily to refocus its strength into an ice-cold twister around Foster and Nixie. After securing a tight shield around them, it burst outwards with all of its strength, sending the ravens into a spinning chaos. The birds smacked against trees and sprawled across the ground—a mess of feathers and beaks—then, each one "poofed" out of existence.

Silence engulfed the clearing as the two fairies crouched back to back, teeth glaring and eyes swiveling in every direction. Lily began to back away from the couple but stopped when she heard the sound of clapping accompanied by laughter rising like a slow boil.

"Bravo, bravo," a male voice called down from a tree to her left. "Congratulations, Foster, on being such a marvelous detective. You have managed to find Oberon's little secret." In a bright red flash, the man jumped from the tree and landed silently in front of the couple. His grin spread from ear to ear as they growled and turned towards him. "Now, now, no reason to be so nasty. We all know how this battle will end so why not just relax. Take a moment to say your goodbyes while I greet our Lily."

"No! She is mine, Robin!" Foster yelled while letting out a howl before pouncing. With a sigh the red-headed newcomer snapped a finger and a branch swung down from a tree, pinning Foster to the ground. Nixie gasped as she jumped to his side and attempted to calm his snarling.

Lily had frozen still as a statue, but when Robin skipped over to her, she pulled off her necklace and held it out towards him. "I am not going with any of you," she stated with a slight tremble to her words.

Robin smiled gently at her before taking a bow, his bright red hair flopping back and forth with every move of his head. "Allow me to introduce myself princess, I am Robin Goodfellow, but you may call me Puck." He reached down to his outfit, an odd array of green leaves, orange flowers, and black feathers; and plucked a lily from a leg of his shorts.

Then he held it out to her, "I've been growing these especially for you. I knew we'd be bound to meet some day. Oberon's blood does tend to attract danger, and whom else would he send to save you but me?" His grin grew even wider as Lily hesitantly reached out and accepted the flower.

"Why you...why...I don't know what's going on. There's two of them..."

"Yes, two of them and just me...little ol' me." His emerald eyes sparkled.

Behind him Nixie whimpered then pleaded, "Just take her and let us go already! If you do, I promise...I'll...I'll owe you one." She choked out the words as if they were bile.

"Shhh..." Robin raised a finger to his lips and sent a large leaf to cling tightly over Nixie's mouth. Then he refocused on Lily. "You see, the strength of the fey comes from the dreams of mankind. The more people who know about and dream about a certain type of fairy, the stronger that fairy becomes."

"Oh...and you're...Puck..." Lily said, barely audibly, as she twirled the flower in her hand.

"Shakespeare's one and only, at your service!" He laughed and spun in a circle. "Now why don't you go somewhere else while I take care of these two enemies of Summer. No sense in you witnessing this grotesqueness."

Lily didn't even pause to think. She kicked off her heels, turned her back on the screams of the man she had thought she loved, and ran as fast as her legs would carry her, heedless of branches scraping at her skin and tearing her dress. At first her lungs burned and her feet ached but eventually her gait grew steady, the ground smoothed beneath her feet, and the brambles in her path slid out of the way. No longer hindered by the forest around her and despite the terror she had left behind, a smile grew on her face and laughter bubbled in her chest.

Seconds later she realized she wasn't alone. Turning her head she saw Puck next to her, keeping pace. "Hello again, Lily." He breathed easy as they ran. "Where are we going?"

"Home," she stated simply as she smiled at him. "Back to my father, he can keep me safe."

"Yes, he can," he responded, "but you know that statement has more than one meaning."
Lily stopped suddenly, the fairy effortlessly stopped alongside. "What are you talking about?" She placed her hands on her hips.

Puck grinned, sunlight glinting in his eyes. "You have a choice now that you've seen. You can come with me, back to the Summer Court and be a princess. Oberon would like to meet you. He has always wondered if you would have your mother's eyes."

"My mother," Lily murmured as she fingered the chain around her neck. The iron chain, fairy poison... her mother's favorite piece of jewlery. "No, I have a home already...and a father." She stated resolutely.

"Very well." He nodded solemnly and with a wave of his hand the trees parted to a clearing where she saw flashlight beams of light and heard dogs barking. Dogs she knew, her father's dogs. "I'll be around, if things should change."

"Yes, thank you," she said absentmindedly as she turned to run into the clearing. The second she broke through the tree line the dogs pounced on her, surrounding her in slobbery tongues and excited "yips".

Laughing, she rolled around with the dogs until a pair of strong hands grabbed her arms and pulled her to his chest. Tears streamed down her face as she breathed in pine sap and felt the rumble of his chest while he choked out, "I thought I had lost you to *them* forever."

"I'm sorry, dad. I'm so sorry." She mumbled into his shirt. Before turning her eyes to where she had just come from.

The path was still visible and on it a dozen pairs of yellow eyes were blinking into view. Her father's dogs began growling. Lily's chest overflowed with anger, she bared her teeth and instinctively waved her hand at the trees. The forest responded rapidly and seconds later, where the path used to be, there was nothing left but a solid wall of green.

"People think I enjoy arguing, but I don't. I'd be much happier if everyone would just agree with me."

-    *Dan Hovseth*

When Dragons Fly
by Amanda Hovseth

"Once upon a time," she recited under her breath, to keep herself distracted while leaping over streams of liquid fire, "there was a *perfect* little summer village with *perfect* little villagers."

She wiped the back of her hand across her sweaty forehead, leaving a streak of volcanic ash over her light purple toned skin.

"But nothing is truly perfect," she continued, "the village had a flaw."

The higher she climbed, the more the air around her seemed to dance, pulling her long, silky silver hair in haphazard twists and spins.

"It lived in the shadow of a massive volcano, and yet, that was not its flaw. Elves of summer do not fear the heat, they use it to grow tropical greenery and bathe in hot water springs. Its flaw was what lived *inside* the volcano."

Lilac pulled herself up on a ledge and gasped for air. To her left stood a jet-black flag, preserved for ages by the wizard's magic. On it was stamped in red letters, "Do Not Enter," his final warning to the few adventurous elves who dared to climb this high.

"Every year the villagers must gather the best of their crops and wealth to sacrifice to the dragon within." She leaned back against the stone and squinted up into the ash-filled sky. "Every year the brave and selfless wizard gathers the payment and delivers it to the dragon, hoping it will be enough." The mountain growled around her. "It is never enough. The wizard always returns in shame and must ask for the first-born of the new year to be sacrificed as well. With this one sacrifice, the rest of the village may prosper—for one more year."

Lilac gracefully shuffled sideways—past the warning flag—and twisted her neck to peek into the massive cave, beyond the jagged walls. Between the smoke and the ash, she could only see a few feet in.

"Once upon a time," she muttered again as she closed her eyes and pictured her sister's joy when—after years of miscarriages—her baby boy was finally born. Then, not long after, came the all-consuming darkness which filled the room when the wizard stepped in.

"I am sorry child," he had said with a low raspy drawl, "I fear yours has beat the others to his first breath." Lilac's sister had screamed in agony and clutched her son to her chest.

The wizard lowered his eyes to the floor before adding, "You may have one full day with him," then he swept out of the room in a flurry of robes.

It was the first time Lilac had ever seen the wizard up close, otherwise she may have noticed sooner, or at least suspected. Immediately after he had left the building, she had started her trek up the side of the roaring mountain.

Of course, she wasn't the first to try to slay the beast, but she was the first of her kind. The others had been trained in warfare and battle, while she was trained in history. The others were boisterous and strong. She was always lost in thought and frail.

Lilac breathed in deep and fought off the cough as she thought over the facts once more. *A wizard, a beast. Slay the beast and the wizard no longer needs to collect. My nephew will live.*

Lilac stepped into the cave. As she walked further and further in, the air began to clear, and the smoke was replaced with a moldy steam.

She had seen the dragon many times. He periodically flew over the city, roaring and smoldering, but he never harmed a soul. This is how she had come to believe in the sacrifice. They all feared the day when the dragon would rain his fury on everyone. It was unfortunate, because, from her studies of history, dragons were hermits, old and wise.

Only rarely, would one turn savage. They are meant to be part of the fey world, not enemies of it.

"You should not have come here child," the wizard's oily voice pierced through the darkness, "I cannot protect you from the dragon once you've entered his territory."

Slay the beast, my nephew lives. She repeated as she used her glamour to produce two long elegant purple swords, one for each hand. Then she stepped out into a glowing cavern and was immediately slammed against a wall by large, scale-covered tail.

I may have made a huge miscalculation, she thought as she frantically thrashed around, failing to pierce the scales with her swords. *Stop!* she chastised herself, *focus!* Then she forced her swords to vanish and said out loud, "Resist for a moment and forever be freed."

In that instant the tail slackened it's hold slightly, allowing her to slide out from behind it. As she hit the ground, she rolled to her feet and took off in a full sprint, weaving in and out of giant gold-cuffed legs and pointed wings. She reproduced her swords before sliding back underneath the dragon's belly. While laying against the warm stones, she took in her surroundings.

Time was of the essence. Hopefully, he hadn't yet noticed she had gotten loose.

Quickly rolling out from underneath the dragon, she stood and lunged forward. Putting all her force behind her swords, she shoved them through the wizard's cloak-covered back.

The ancient man gasped and fell to his knees, clutching at his chest. He turned towards her. "Why?" He wheezed out.

Lilac scrambled backwards, out of reach. Then she said, "Slay the beast, save my nephew."

The wizard's expression changed from surprise to rage. "How dare you!" He growled as he mustered up the strength to cast one last spell.

Lilac ducked into the fetal position as the waves of lethal energy moved towards her, but before they could hit, a large wing wrapped around her body, shielding her from the attack.

As the wizard took his last shuddering breath, the golden cuffs around the dragon's legs clanked to the ground.

*"I don't care what other people do. Other people do dumb
things all the time, doesn't mean you have to do it."*

-    *Dan Hovseth*

Countdown to Clarity
by Giles Hovseth

Five officers sprinted down roads lit only by dim
yellows and flashing blues and reds. The monster
would not escape from them. The monster could not
escape from them. Soon the shade would give way to
blinding white, and the monster would be found. The
monster would be cornered.

Four shots had been fired. None had found their
mark in the deep brown bark that would give way to
the cold sheen of the brass. Instead they had landed
in spots pale and unintended. Their new home
accused them of wrongdoing, but they had only
gotten a little lost.

Three EMTs worked to dam a river of crimson.
They knew they could not stem the tide. White gave
way…gave way…gave way.

Two brothers dashed in different directions, running to the same end. Their mother was left alone in waves of blue.

One gun ended two lives in three seconds for five minutes of fun.

Black.

"I'd just nuke them all."

Dan Hovseth

Life and Legacy
by Amanda Hovseth

Red. Blue. Red. Blue. Red. Blue.

Gracie's eyesight blurred as she watched the police lights flash against the wall in front of her. Clinging to the paper clip which had saved her life, she tried with all her might to squish herself further underneath her receptionist desk.

Red. Blue. Red. Blue.

Just minutes earlier she had been laughing with her co-worker, Janet-the-Scientist.

Janet had made a joke. "Do you know what smallpox said to the elderly scientist?"

"No, what?"

"Turn the heat down, you're killing me! Hah! Get it? Because smallpox causes fevers but the elderly like it so hot even viruses can't handle it! Haha!"

Gracie had laughed along—to be polite.

Red. Blue. Red. Blue.

65

Then Gracie had dropped her paperclip and the little bastard had bounced itself to the farthest recesses of the space underneath her desk.

Blue. Red. Blue. Red.

At some point shortly after those embarrassing moments of dropping to her knees and sidling after the cheeky little jerk, gunshots were fired, and Janet's lifeless body had fallen across Gracie's desk chair.

Red. Blue. Re—

Gracie's eyes drifted from the wall to the blood drizzling off of Janet's hand.

Red. Red. Red.

Something heavy and metallic slammed onto the desk above her. Gracie squeezed her hand over her mouth.

"How are the cops already here?"

"Relax! They won't breach until they are sure we don't have hostages. By then, the virus will be released, and they will spread it for us."

Calm down, Gracie, she thought to herself. *They don't know you're here. As soon as they get through the door you can run outside.* She turned her gaze to the wall. *Red. Blue. Red. Blue.*

"I'm in!"

The door squeaked open and three sets of footsteps marched through.

Just wait a little longer. She encouraged herself. *Soon they will turn the corner towards the labs and you'll be free. Red. Blue. Red. Blue. The labs...the bio labs...Red. Red. Red.*

Gracie crept to the edge of the desk and poked her head up. She choked down a sob as she counted the bodies lying throughout the lobby.

Five, five plus Janet. Janet. The labs. Gracie took a deep breath. *It's now or never.* She sprang to her feet and took two quick steps towards the front door. *Red. Blue. Red. Blue.* Then she promptly tripped on one of Janet's stray high-heeled shoes and went sprawling across the floor.

Gasping, she whipped around to gaze down the hallway. *Red. Red. Red.* Luckily no one was in sight. She sighed.

At this point her entire body was involuntarily shaking. She braced herself against the wall and gingerly rose to a standing position. As her fingers relaxed against the embossed lettering of a wall sign, the paperclip fell from her grip and bounced itself into the hallway—towards the labs.

Gracie watched its foolish trajectory and then raised her eyes to read the sign. A sign she had read a million times but had never given much thought to.

Restricted Area
Biohazard
Authorized Personnel Only
Red. Red. Red. Well. Dammit!

Gracie took a deep breath, grabbed Janet's heel, and began stumbling her way along the path set by that dickhead of a paperclip.

As she reached the hall which led towards the labs, she pressed herself against the wall and carefully peeked around the corner. Ten feet ahead on her left, one of the doors was wide open. Angry bickering was trailing out.

"You should be on the lookout!"

"Everyone's dead!"

"Get your dumb ass out in the hallway and do your job!"

Gracie froze in place. *It's now or never, all in or all out.* She thought of Janet, brilliant, but so dumb when it came to people. *Still, she loved people, she'd never want her work to be used for ill...* She thought of her father, killed by an IED while serving his third tour with the Marines. His words ran through her head: *"Eventually, we all die, might as well be while giving our best."* Gracie gripped the high-heeled shoe tighter, rounded the corner, and picked up her pace. She reached the open door just as one of the men came angrily stomping out. *Red. Red. Red.*

Before he even knew she was there, she leapt at him. The man's head slammed into the hard tile flooring and the pair went sliding across the shiny white ground.

From inside the doorway came a stream of cursing.

"Who the hell was that?"

She knew she had to hurry. She raised Janet's shoe into the air and slammed the pointed heal into the man's eye. The man screamed in agony as she leaned all her weight onto the shoe and felt it slide further and further into his skull. Then she quickly pulled the AR-15 from his dying grasp and rolled off him into a kneeling position while hoisting the gun to her shoulder—like her father had shown her many times. Then she waited.

Red. Red. Red.

"What is going o—" a man bellowed as he stepped into the hallway. He promptly took two bullets to the chest and one to the forehead.

Gracie stood up and slid the dead man out of the doorway. *Red. Red. Red.* Then she briskly marched into the lab and slammed the door so hard it knocked a wall thermometer off its nail.

"You're too late! I've already released the virus!" the remaining man bellowed as he raised his gun.

Gracie bent down to pick up the thermometer. She traced her thumb along the top of the red liquid. *Red. Red. Red. Seventy-eight degrees.* Full of resolve, she calmly turned and shot the handle off the door—the only exit from the lab.

The man put two bullets into her gut.

Gracie dropped to her knees and asked him, "Do you know what smallpox said to the elderly scientist?"

Then she unloaded her magazine into the nearby oxygen tanks, engulfing the lab in flames.

Red. Red. Red.

"No matter how weird or boring someone seems, if you ask them enough questions about themselves, you can find at least one thing about them that's interesting enough for you to learn to enjoy their company."

- *Dan Hovseth*

Unearthing Memories
by Amanda Hovseth

"They say it's impossible."

"Who says it's impossible?"

"I don't know, 'they'." He made finger quotes.

"There's always a 'they' isn't there." She mimicked.

"Well, yes, but it doesn't mean they're wrong."

"It doesn't mean they're right." The grandfather clock in the corner ticked away the seconds as the pair sat in silence. "Why should we care what they think anyway?"

"That's easy for you to say. You've never cared what anybody thinks."

"What's that supposed to mean?" She sat forward, adjusting her notebook, and using her pen to push her glasses up her nose.

"It's just..." He rearranged his lounging position so he could get a better look at the girl in the photograph resting on the table beside him. "You've always been so brave...so...certain of who you are. I don't have that luxury."

"Why not?"

He blurred his vision so he could imagine her lips forming those words. "You know why not, Cindy, because I can't remember."

"You can't remember? Or you choose not to remember?"

"No, no, no!" He reached out and knocked the photograph over. "She wouldn't have said that."

The woman with the tight white bun on the top of her head sighed and asked, "What would she have said then?"

He placed his right hand on his forehead and rolled to stare at the ceiling. "I don't know...just not that...never that."

"Why not that?"

"She wouldn't want me to remember."

"How do you know?"

"Because she loved me."

The woman reached out, grabbed an opaque pitcher, and filled a glass of water. He watched as the green lamp on the table sent sparks of light bouncing off the flowing liquid. "Would you like some?" she asked him.

"No, I'm not thirsty."

"If she wouldn't have asked you that, then how about I ask you?" She took a sip of her water. "Do you think it's possible that you may simply be choosing not to remember?"

"Of course not, why wouldn't I want to remember?"

"You tell me."

"They say I can't remember."

"Why do they say that?"

"Because the brain doesn't heal like that. It can't re-form pieces it has lost." He waved his right hand around his head.

"But what if it hasn't lost everything you think it has?"

"How would I know that?"

"You wouldn't."

"I'll have a glass of water now."

She filled him a cup and handed it over. He lifted the picture back to its standing position then closed his eyes and drank slowly as he tried to recall the sound of her voice, the teasing way she used to nudge his shoulder, the way her eyes slowly grew blank as her last breath eased out of her lips…Water poured down the front of his shirt as his eyes shot open. Coughing, he jumped to his feet and turned his back on the woman.

"Henry, what is it? What happened?" She asked, tapping a pen on her notebook, and glancing at her reflection in a mirror on the wall to her right.

"They say it's impossible."

"Why don't you sit back down, Henry. I'll get you a towel to dry off."

He sat on the edge of the couch, his face turned away from the photograph, as he reached up by his left ear and scratched under the bandage that was wrapped around his head.

"It's their fault you know, if they hadn't have shot me I could remember everything. I could tell you anything." He accepted the towel and began twisting it in his hands.

"When you think of her, what sort of smells come to mind? Anything stand out?"

He closed his eyes again and breathed deeply, "Yes, her perfume...so fresh, so pure..."

"Anything else?"

"It's kind of...strange..." He wrinkled his nose.

"Strange is fine, everything connected to her is important to you, so I would like to hear it."

"...well, I smell...it smells kind of like dirty animals. Like wet dog but...not a dog..." he shook his head.

"That's good, what about sounds? Do you hear anything?"

The clock ticked louder as she glanced at the mirror again.

"Yes!" He practically shouted as he slapped his hand on the armrest. "A roar, like a lion's yawn. She loved lions! We used to go see the lions!" He opened his eyes and grinned.

"You would take her to the zoo?"

"Yes, well…no. There was this path behind the zoo we would walk on. I would help her climb the trees and we'd sit on a branch which was high enough to see past the walls." He laughed and picked up the photograph, stroking his thumb down her brown hair.

"The path behind the zoo? On the side by the lion's cage?" The woman eyed the mirror again before leaning forward. "Now, Henry this may seem like a weird question, and it may be hard to consider. But I would greatly appreciate it if you would try your best to think it through."

He continued stroking the photograph.

"When was that photograph taken?"

"It was in High School, her Senior photo. The year we met."

"You love her, don't you?"

"Yes, more than anything."

"What would happen if you lost her?"

He pulled his eyes from the photo and narrowed them in her direction. "Why would I lose her? Has something happened?"

"No, I'm sorry Henry, I didn't mean to alarm you. This is just theoretical, so I can understand how much you love her."

He nodded and set the photograph down.

"She liked the lions?"

"Yes."

"If she died what would she want to happen with her body?"

"Cremation, she's scared of being buried alive."

"Cremation, yes, then what?"

"That's easy, I would take her ashes to our tree and bury them there, so she could always watch the lions."

The woman smiled, set down her clipboard, and turned to the mirror before saying. "The tree behind the zoo, overlooking the lion's cage. Sounds like the perfect spot for you to remember your loved one."

The front page of the next morning's newspaper was both heartbreaking and a relief. "Remains of Five Missing Girls Found." Below the title was a row of photographs: all young women, all brunette, and all smiling.

"Everyone's an asshole. Some people just learn to hide it better."

-      *Dan Hovseth*

Rage
by Amanda Hovseth

June 7, 2014

People often ask me how I did it, how I could survive such a trauma… Even if they don't ask, I can see it in their eyes. Staring at me, tracing the lines of my body up and down with no fear of what they may uncover. They are lucky I have composed my shell so well.

My husband was a business lawyer. It was a stressful job and he needed to be able to relax at the end of the day, so he could take care of us all. It's not easy having the entire financial burden of a family on one's head. When the kids had first started grade school I offered to get a day job, but it was silly of me. I would have never been able to handle such a task. At least John got a good laugh out of it, he was positively chipper for the rest of the evening.

My two children are off at college now, twins, one boy and one girl. The poor things were barely out of the house when their father passed, "suicide" they labeled it. I've been told I was the one who found him in our old living room with a bullet hole through his skull. But, all I remember is grabbing my purse to go buy some more Blue Moon. He was drinking the last one, and it's never good to run out. Then, suddenly, I was shading my eyes from flashing red and blue lights, being asked all sorts of questions, and wondering why my jaw ached.

"Very good, Mrs. Marlow. How do you feel about this writing exercise?" He set her russet colored journal, with its manufactured cracked leather cover, down on the glass topped coffee table between them.

"I think I'm enjoying it. I haven't gotten much finished though, as you can see." She leaned forward, motioning towards the journal, which caused her pressed white dress to wrinkle at the waist and her frosted brown hair bun to let loose a few strands. "But, I do think writing paired quite nicely with my morning coffee."

"Well this is certainly a great start." The young man seated across from her had black hair, parted right down the middle, and it shined in the soft glow of the table lamp to his right. He sniffed and pushed his glasses higher up on his nose.

Mrs. Marlow smiled at the motion, he had been doing that since the first day he was saddled with a pair in the fourth grade. Ainsley "Lee" McSwain had grown up right down the street from her old home, and even though he was a few years older than her own children, his stunted height and lack of social skills placed him in their friend group. The three of them used to spend their summer days roaming the neighborhood, kicking cans, and hitting baseballs until the street lights came on and her husband whistled loudly out the door.

"What is it that has you smiling, Mrs. Marlow?" asked the now grown-up version of the boy, with oiled brown shoes on his feet and a college psychology diploma framed on the wall.

"I'm just remembering that night you brought flowers to my little Bambi." She grabbed a tissue from the table in front of her and dabbed the corners of her eyes. "You were so adorable in your button up shirt with hair all combed back. Do you remember that day?"

Lee's freckled face turned bright red. He tapped his pen on his notebook and cleared his throat. "Yes ma'am, I remember. But it's not me we should be talking about—"

"Oh poo," she flicked her wrist in his direction, causing the tissue to trail lazily after. "You're just embarrassed. Well, no reason to be embarrassed, I say. My Bambi was very young and unsure of what she wanted. Have you talked to her lately?"

He uncrossed his legs and sat up straighter. "As a matter of fact, I have. She called to ask me how our sessions were going. Naturally, I had to remind her about doctor-patient confidentiality."

"I'm still on your side, you know. What is it kids say nowadays…oh yes, Team Ainsley!" She punched her hand into the air and waved her tissue around.

He laughed lightly. "Thank you, Mrs. Marlow... but tell me..." He readjusted the clipboard on his arm rest. "What do you think Mr. Marlow's opinion about Bambi's options would have been?"

"Dear, dear boy, who could have said what that man ever thought...and what does it matter now?" She coughed softly, grinned again, and dabbed at her eyes. "I do find I miss him though. Some days my apartment is just too quiet."

"Well, if you don't mind my asking, you say here, and I quote, 'They are lucky I have composed my shell so well.'" He tapped her journal with his pen. "What is it that this shell is hiding?"

She sighed loudly. "Nothing really I suppose, it's just...you know...poetry."

"Right, yes, but it does seem to be talking about a tangible reality."

"Of course it's a reality. Isn't it a reality for everyone? I'm sure even you have something to hide."

"Perhaps, and yet we aren't here to talk about other people's shells, we are here to talk about yours." He raised his eyebrows and pursed his lips. "What is your shell hiding?"

"Maybe if you opened up to Bambi, let her see beneath your shell..."

"Mrs. Marlow—" He pulled out a slightly damp, light green handkerchief and dabbed his forehead. "Like I've said, we're not here to talk about my secrets."

She simply shrugged her shoulders and twisted the tissue between her hands. "I'm just saying maybe she'll be impressed by certain secret—grateful even."

"What type of secret could possibly make her grateful?"

Mrs. Marlow reached into her purse and pulled out what looked like a child's, handmade friendship bracelet, only longer and not tied in a circle. It was an intricate weave of red, blue, and green. She rubbed it between her forefinger and thumb while lightly biting her lower lip. "This was his you know."

"His?"

"My late husband's, he used it as a strap for his reading glasses. Bambi made it for him when she was in the fourth grade."

Lee scratched his nose and shifted in his seat before softly saying, "She must have loved him." He cleared his throat.

Her light green eyes appeared to fog over, reminding Lee of clouds rumbling over the sea. She stared off behind his head while saying, "I caught her trying to burn it once. She was in high school." Her gaze shifted down to the strap. "I should have let her do it."

"Why do you say that?"

"I made her put it back. He caught her touching his glasses and…" She sniffed and closed her eyes, then sat there silently for a few seconds before letting out a long breath. "He was wearing this the day he died… Do you remember?"

Lee was staring at the strap, his fingers turning white from gripping his pen.

Mrs. Marlow smiled gently. "Ainsley dear?" He tore his eyes from their task, sat back, and set his pen down. She watched the blood ease back into his fingers before she asked, "Have you spoken to Barrett lately?"

He cleared his throat, crossed his legs, and answered, "Yes, Mrs. Marlow, I speak to him almost every day. In fact, right after our session ends—" He lifted his pocket watch up, causing its chain to jingle. "In about two minutes, we will be meeting to play poker."

"Oh good." A shining smile filled her face. "Do give him my love and make sure to tell him, I truly am happy now. And no matter what, he will always be my little boy!"

"Yes, of course." He shifted sideways in his seat and bit his thumbnail while glancing at the strap, which was now resting on top of Mrs. Marlow's purse, on her lap. "Actually, would you mind terribly if I excused myself to use the restroom?"

"Not at all." She stood quickly, knocking her purse to the floor. "It's always great to see you darling," she added while sweeping lipstick, a compact, a blue journal, the eyeglass strap, and various shiny items back into her purse.

"You as well, Mrs. Marlow." He smiled and stood up to shake her hand.

When she straightened, she looped her purse strap over her shoulder and clasped his hand in hers. "Mind if I grab one last cup of tea for my trip home?"

He squeezed their handshake with his left hand, said, "Help yourself," then headed towards the bathroom, calling over his shoulder, "see you next week Mrs. Marlow."

June 9th, 2014

I have a place of my own now. A nice little apartment overlooking the bay. I like to sit on my window seat—Bambi embroidered it with lilacs for me—and watch the waves converse with the shore. It's different every day. Some days they roar in, foaming with fury until they crash hard on the shining shells, dragging monstrous stones and torn kelp in their wake, creating a dented and unkempt beach. Other days they approach with a whisper, slipping in gifts of sparkling sea glass as they kiss the sand in shame for their past rampage. But it never lasts, soon enough the sea will rage, sending uproarious waves and destroying all of the hope and beauty it had once promised to maintain. I never know what to anticipate. In some ways the inconsistency is comforting—expected. I suppose that's my "broken" talking.

"Hello, mother."

Mrs. Marlow dropped her pen and spun her head towards the noise, gasping loudly before she realized it was her son standing behind her.

"Oh my!" She placed one hand over her heart and began using the other to fan her face. "Barrett! You startled me."

The left side of his mouth turned up while he shook his head and pushed her russet colored journal farther back on the seat, so he could sit next to her by the window. "Sorry, I didn't mean to. I thought you would've heard me. Maybe you should start locking your door if it's that easy for someone to sneak up."

She waved her hand at him and took in a deep breath before letting it out slowly. "What does an old lady like me have to fear of open doors?"

Barrett frowned. "Mom! Lots of things could happen! You'd be crazy easy to rob…what could you do against robbers?"

"If they want it they can have it." She swept an arm around her apartment in a grand gesture then brought it around to rest on her son's shoulder. "Did you come by just to make certain my door was locked?"

"No." He leaned sideways and rested his forehead against the window pane. "I just wanted to talk to you… to ask you about the day dad died."

His mother turned and stared out the window while picking up her journal and moving it to the floor. "What would you want to dwell on that for?"

He watched as her eyes traced the path a wave left across the sand. "It's just…I don't know if…I'm not sure I believe he would kill himself."

"Barrett? Dear boy, it's been years! Have you been thinking that this entire time?"

"No…I had a dream about dad a month ago and I just can't get it out of my head. He was just always so...well you know...tough, I guess. Why would he kill himself?"

"Why would someone else kill him?"

Barrett furrowed his brow and narrowed his eyelids as he made eye contact with his mother. They sat studying each other for a full fifteen seconds. She took in his broad shoulders and sharp cheek bones, so much like his father's, and he noticed her rounded nose, slightly bent in the middle from one of her many clumsy mishaps.

Finally, Barrett sighed and said, "Mother...mom, I mean, I don't know. He could have gotten in a fight at a bar. Maybe someone from work...maybe someone he had hurt...somehow."

She smiled gently and placed a hand on his knee. "What if someone did kill him? What then? Would you hunt them down?"

"Yeah, probably." He shrugged.

"Then say you found her...or him. Then what? Would you turn them in to the cops?" Barrett leaned back against the window and crossed his arms. "Would you kill them yourself?" She leaned in close to whisper into his ear. "Or would you thank them?"

Barrett jumped up and spun to face her. "Thank them! Why on earth would I thank someone for murdering my father?"

She sighed and turned to stare at the waves, raising one hand to rub her jaw. "Why, indeed?"

"Mom?" He paced back and forth. "Mom! What are you even looking at?"

"Hmmm...Oh nothing, sorry dear." She turned to face him. "Have you seen your sister lately?"

"Ugh, mom I..." He stopped, grasped his right elbow with his left hand and reached up to run his fingers through his sun bleached, ear length hair. "I...yeah, yeah I have. I saw her last night."

His mother smiled. "Good! What were the two of you up to?"

"Nothing really." He shrugged then sat back down beside her. "I didn't even expect her to stop by. Lee and I were hanging out at my place and she just showed up. It was kind of weird actually."

"How so?" She tilted her head to the side.

"She barely acknowledged me. Just walked in and asked if she could speak to Lee privately. They talked for...I don't know how long, I actually fell asleep on the couch waiting for him to come back, and when I woke up there was a note saying he'd catch me later."

"Really?" She grinned widely, causing him to furrow his brow.

"Why are you smiling? What's going on?"

"Nothing, nothing." She rubbed her chin and grinned even wider.

"You think they hooked up!" He sat up straight and his eyes widened. "You *want* them to hook up?"

"Phooey, I just want Bambi to be safe...and happy. Safe and happy, it's all I've ever wanted for the two of you." She dropped her gaze to the floor to trace the lines on the carpet that were left from vacuuming. "I just regret not being able to give that to you myself."

"And you think Lee can keep her safe? Scrawny little Lee?"

She looked back at him and raised an eyebrow. "He's already proven himself, hasn't he?"

"What? How?"

She just shrugged, smiled, and turned towards the waves again.

"Are you talking about that time on the boardwalk?" She didn't respond. "That time those guys were harassing her, so he punched one in the face?" Still no response. "Mom…yeah, that was chivalrous of him and whatever, but he still got his ass whooped… mom? Mother?"

"Yes, dear?" Her eyes stayed glued to the waves.

"What could you possibly be looking…mom! Can you at least *look* at me?"

She spun her face towards him quickly, but her eyes dragged over slowly as if they were pulling an anchor from the sea. "He was there the night your father passed."

"I know. He heard the gunshot and came running."

"I don't remember when he arrived, but I do remember him convincing the police to give me a break, and he stayed by my side until you and Bambi returned."

He shook his head slightly. "He's a good guy, no objection there. I just don't think he's Bambi's type."

She smiled at him and reached out to touch his cheek. "Types are illusions, a cage of thorns weaved by our own hands while we pretend we are actually surrounded by roses."

Barrett snorted, took her hand from his cheek, and squeezed it gently. "Thorns or not, all Bambi's boyfriends have been more like dad and less like poor Ainsley."

His mother flinched and retracted her hand before quickly smiling and reaching up to tousle his hair around. "Who knows, things could be happening, illusions can change…we will just have to wait and see."

He shook his head, returned her smile, and reached an arm over to give her a side hug. "I have to go, or I'll be late for work."

"Okay dear. Love you."

"Love you too, mom." He stood up and walked from the room. She heard her front door open before he called out again. "And don't forget to lock your door!"

She sighed and turned back to the waves.

…I wish I could tell her everything. I wish I could tell her that she's free now because of me. Her chestnut hair can shine gold in the sun without fear of ever being snuffed out again. But would it bring us closer, or would she hate me? I can't stand the thought of her hating me. How am I supposed to live like this? In the shadows, the truth lost to time…

The words blurred together through the tears in her eyes, so Bambi turned from the royal blue journal, closing it gently while running her fingers across its smooth surface. It wasn't the first time she had read it, she already knew what it said, had returned to it over and over again since the night she had slipped it out of his office. She unrolled some toilet paper, folded it over a couple of times, and blew her nose into it. Then, after checking her reflection in the mirror, she straightened her shoulders and walked from the florescent lights of the bathroom into the dusky bar. Blinking a few times, she tossed her hair back and set a straight course towards her target.

"Lee…Ainsley," She called out as she stepped up behind him, but her voice trailed off amongst the blaring of the speakers. She sighed and shifted her weight to her left leg, then reached out and touched his shoulder.

Lee practically choked on the white wine he was drinking. "Bambi…Bambi! What's up?" He spun his bar stool around and wiped his mouth with his shirt sleeve.

"Who drinks wine at a place like this? Really, Lee."

"I…Oh, umm…" He reached around and set his glass on the table.

"Never mind." She grabbed his hand, pulling him to his feet. "I need to talk to you again."

"To talk? Yeah...yes of course..." He stumbled after her into the empty street, shivering slightly at the brisk night air. "Where are we going?"

Turning abruptly, she whisked the journal out of her purse and into his hand. "I don't want to play games anymore. I just want you to tell me the truth. Right now."

Lee stood with his back against the dingy brick wall of the bar. Dulled music pounded through the stones. "Where'd you get this? Did your mom give you one of her journals?"

"My mom? What? No! That's your journal, I took it from a desk drawer in your office."

"Mine? I don't have a...you went through my desk?"

"Yes."

"W...why?"

She groaned and turned sideways, crossing her arms and gripping her elbows. "I don't know, I thought...I was talking on the phone with my mom the other day and she said something about you and...I didn't believe her, but she insisted I look into it..." Tears welled up in her eyes, so she turned her back on him to wipe them away.

"Bambi?" He stepped forward and put a hand on her shoulder turning her towards him. "What's going on? What's the matter? Is it something I did?"

She shook her head rapidly, causing her silky-smooth hair to brush over his hand and the smell of her shampoo to tickle his nose. He breathed in deep.

"You tell me Lee." She wiped her eyes with the cuff of her dress sleeve then fixed him with her toughest stare while motioning towards the journal. "*Did* you do something?"

He retracted his hand and eyed her curiously as he opened up the journal, then he began to read.

Bambi took a few steps away to lean against a lamppost, the angle of the light masking her eyes in shadow and causing her red lips to shimmer as they pressed together in a frown.

After a few seconds Lee peered at her over the rims of his glasses. "You found this in my desk? In *my* office? I assume this was your real intent then, that night you came to Barrett's apartment and asked if you could borrow one of my textbooks?"

She placed a hand on her hip and admitted between clenched teeth, "Mom told me you had a journal, and where she'd seen you put it."

He furrowed his brow, shook his head, and closed the journal, rubbing his thumb along the spine.

"Is…is there something you need to tell me?" Her voice cracked as she pushed herself off the lamppost and stood up straight.

He watched her for a few seconds, while silently rocking back and forth.

"Ugh! Really?" She reached up with both hands, grabbed her hair in two big clumps and began pulling on it. "Say something already! I basically already know anyway!"

"Know what?" He reached out gently, attempting to remove her hands from the tangle of hair. She shuddered and stepped away from him, nearly tripping over the base of the lamppost.

"This is all my fault isn't it? My father is dead because of me!"

"What? No! Bambi, come on, let's get you back to your apartment. I think you've had too much to drink." He wrapped an arm around her waist and began pulling her towards the subway station.

"Don't patronize me *Ainsley*, I haven't even had one drink today." She shoved him off, crossed her arms, and clenched her jaw.

He raised his hands in surrender. "Okay, okay then." He readjusted his glasses. "Tell me, why is it your fault your father killed himself?"

She snorted, then let loose a stream of anxiety in one breathless admitting, "Yeah, killed himself. Killed himself only a few days after you found me crying in our old tree house. Killed himself after I revealed all my most horrific secrets to you that night. Killed himself for no damn reason! No one kills themselves for no reason!" She paused and gulped in air. "I saw the way you looked that night. I had never seen you angrier. Your outrage was practically tangible." She raised up her right hand and wiggled her fingers around as if molding clay. Then she hiccupped and temporarily covered her mouth, before softly adding, "You killed him because I told you what he had done to me."

Lee removed his glasses to rub his nose between his thumb and fore-finger, and walked back to lean against the wall. He tilted his head and stared up at the blank night sky, imagining the stars which he was too blind to see. Then he held the journal out to her. "I didn't write this. I've never even seen this journal before."

She guffawed, and pointed at the bottom corner of the back cover. "It's engraved with your initials."

He replaced his glasses and glanced at the initials. "That doesn't mean anything. I wasn't even there when he died. I ran to your house when I heard the gunshot and found your mother sitting next to him on the couch."

"Oh! So, you're going to blame my mom now! After everything that man put her through, you want his curse to follow her from the after-life?"

"No! No of course not! I'm just saying…" He groaned then thumped the journal against his chest while he stared at the sky and turned in a circle. "He was already dead when I got there."

She reached into her bag, pulled out the handmade eyeglass strap, waved it in front of his eyes, and said, "I'll bet you've never seen this before either then?"

His eyes flicked back and forth, following the red, blue, and green weave. Then he blinked and adjusted his glasses.

"*Have* you *seen* it?"

He sighed. "Yes, your mother showed me it during our last appointment."

She crossed her arms and glared at him. "It was being used as a bookmark in *your* journal, Lee!"

He shook his head and raised a palm out to her in surrender. "Honestly Bambi, I don't know what you want me to say. What is it you want from me?"

"The truth, the truth Lee! That's all I want!"

He slowly bowed his head, rubbed his temple, and closed his eyes. "I am telling you the truth...but fine let's play it your way. What if I did kill him? What then?" He tossed the journal on the ground and his cheeks flushed. He stared at her, cold and hard, she gripped her elbows and shivered, averting her gaze.

"Come on Bambi, don't back down now." He took one step towards her. "Let's say you're right." He took another step. "After all, it is true that what you told me about your father had me outraged. My blood boiled as I saw the pain he put you through." He continued moving toward her, so she backed up until there was no space left between her and someone's dusty red Camry. "So, let's just say, for the time being, that I went home that night after holding you in my arms while you cried yourself to sleep, and began plotting. Then, I waited until you and Barrett left for college because I wouldn't want either of you implicated." He stopped to rub his chin. "Hmmm...maybe I even stole all the beer from your parent's fridge just so I could guarantee your mother would have to leave the house." He was now directly in front of her so she began leaning back. He whispered in her ear, "What did I do then Bambi?"

She swallowed deep and placed the palms of her hands behind her against the hood of the car so she could lean further away.

"What did I do?" He asked again.

"You shot him." It was hardly audible.

"What was that?" He cupped his ear with his hand.

"You shot him!"

"I shot him!" He slammed one fist next to her on the hood of the car. "I shot and killed your father because he was a monster! And you couldn't be free if he was still alive! What now!"

They both froze in place. His face was bright red and he gasped for breath, propped up against the car with the hand he had used to hit it, pinning her in place. Her mascara was running in streams down her cheeks, and her mouth was agape as she fell backwards onto her forearms.

He sighed and shook his head, taking a step back while saying once more, "What now?"

But before he could turn away, her arms were wrapped around his neck pulling him toward her. "I should've done this a long time ago," she whispered against his lips.

June 13th, 2014

Today I grew tired of watching the heartless waves roar without opposition, so I went down to the beach. Some kids must have left their bucket because I found a cute little red one being tossed around in the current. I pulled it ashore and began stuffing it with wet sand. There's an endless supply of it after all, the result of constant bombardment. Then I carried it up above the tide line, where all was untouched, and began to build. Trip after trip I took, dragging fragments of shells and salt soaked dirt up the beach, chafing my palms until it appeared as if the blood beneath my skin shone through. Finally, I was satisfied with the results. My will—forever freed—had sculpted a wonderful sandcastle complete with bridges and a moat, filled with water from the tide. The breeze smelled crisp and promising as I laid back and watched the sun begin to set, my brand-new castle in the foreground and the waves echoing a dying cry from somewhere in the past.

"I wish I would have eaten more."

\-   *Dan Hovseth (on his deathbed)*

The Stranger in the Stairwell

by Giles Hovseth

There was a man who would stand in my apartment building's stairwell. He stood on the floor between floors. I would see him going up, and I would see him going down. I would nod as I walked by. He would nod back, and we would leave it at that.

He was a strange man who wore strange clothing, but he never seemed out of place. Some days he wore a nice black suit with a nice black hat, clean shaven and professional. Other days he wore a bright red tracksuit and worn sneakers that seemed to melt into the floor, his greying beard smoky and crackling as it billowed from his chin.

When it rained, he donned a rain coat with formerly bright yellows, muted from years of use. Beneath the rain coat, he would alternate between the formal dress of an Imperial Navy crewman and the swim trunks of a drunken college freshman on spring break. In either case, his clothes were always drenched beneath the coat, and a puddle spread out beneath him that I would carefully step around.

When it snowed, he wore a fluffy sweater and a Ushanka hat that covered his ears, his face bearing a stark white mustache that pointed dramatically left and right, frozen in time by the natural hair gel of sweat in undesirable places. His shoes were solid and mottled black, perpetually slicked by the drifts of snow he had marched through to get wherever he had gone.

Sometimes he wore scrubs or a doctor's lab coat. A mask would cover his face, but the subtle curve beneath his nose implied a sterile hairlessness intended to ease his breathing, ultimately ineffective in that regard, as air rasped its way around the edges of the mask.

Sometimes, all he wore was a diaper. Other times, all he wore was an animal skin loincloth stained by the blood of whichever beast he had taken it from. And still other times, he seemingly wore nothing at all, cloaked in an eerie darkness, the bulb above him burnt out.

He never seemed out of place. It was as if the stairwell shaped itself to whatever form he had taken that day, as if he were a fixture in the apartment building of equal importance with the stairwell itself.

Everyone in the building had grown accustomed to his eccentric vigil.

When I spoke with my fellow tenants about him, it became clear that he was a stranger to all of us. Nobody had ever talked to him. Nobody had ever asked him who he was, or where he came from. Nobody knew anything about him besides the fact that he stood in the stairwell, day in and day out. They would nod as they walked by, he would nod back, and they would leave it at that, putting thoughts of him aside until the next time they had to visit their neighbors or old friends on different floors.

Naturally, when we discovered that we had an unsolved and unprecedented mystery before us, we gave ourselves over to the fathomless depths of unbound imagination applied to conversation. We could not simply ask the man about himself. That would ruin the mystery. Instead we exchanged ideas and theories, each more wildly complex than the last, and we chose to believe whichever theory we liked best.

Some of us believed that he was simply a man with nowhere else to go. He stood in the stairwell every day and every night because he had nothing better to do than stand and nowhere better to be than here. He walked in one day, and one day he would walk out, and that was that; no need to think about him or discuss him any further because that was all we needed to know. This explanation was enough for some, but others were unsatisfied.

One theory claimed the man was an old friend of the Super's. The Super had wanted some company back when the building was tenantless and opened the doors to the man without knowing or caring how long he intended to stay. With the permission of the Super, the man decided he liked the stairwell and has stood there ever since. The original Super left ages ago, but the man stayed behind.

Some rejected this theory. After all, the Landlord would never allow a strange man to stay in his building for so long. He would scare away the tenants. This problem was met with many different responses. The man had never been kicked out, so the Landlord must have allowed him to stay for some reason. Perhaps the Landlord either did not know or did not care about the man. Perhaps the Landlord had a contract with the old Super allowing the man to stay. Perhaps the building never had a Landlord at all. Perhaps this man was the Landlord, and he stood in the stairwell keeping watch over his building and his tenants.

There were those among us who did not care for talk of the Landlord. They paid their rent, and they paid their dues. A man like that should never be allowed to stand in the stairwell. He was a nuisance and a menace. If the Landlord did not care to evict the man, they would take that duty upon themselves. They talked and talked, and planned and planned, but nothing ever came of their talking, and nothing ever came of their planning. The man stood, unfazed by the hatred some had sent his way, and all their fuming was for naught.

In the end, we could only discuss this strange man with the ignorance befitting a group of cattle mooing near the slaughterhouse. We would never know the answer, and that was fine by me. I enjoyed the debate and the theories and the arguments. I enjoyed thinking about the man. I was content with the world of possibilities that he presented, and my beliefs about him would shift with each new proposal and each new dilemma the others presented. He was all of the fun of a murder mystery with all of the distance of a detective who has no stake in the outcome.

But one day, everything changed.

I was making dinner. The stove was on high, broiling the steak to a nice medium-rare. A pan was frying two eggs, over-easy. I had hash browns and toast (with a side of butter and jelly) already cooked, waiting to be eaten. A half-gallon of milk, a pitcher of orange juice, and a bottle of iced coffee sat in the fridge. It was to be a delicious supper, one perfectly fitting the torrential downpour occurring just outside my kitchen window. Then, I heard a sharp knock crack at my door, as lightning flashed through the sky.

I hadn't invited anyone over. I hadn't ordered anything in the mail. I hadn't had a door-to-door salesman ever knock before. This knock was entirely unexpected, but I opened the door nonetheless.

The man stood at my doorstep, fist raised to knock again. He wore a jacket that appeared to be sewn out of sheets of copper. His hair and beard were charcoal black and stuck out straight, pointing in all different directions. When he breathed, his clothes would ripple and shift with his chest, lines in the fabric shimmering in bursts of light that seemed to spark from his flesh.

He had left the stairwell. For the first time in my life, I was seeing the man in an environment altogether alien to his presence. He was at my doorstep, and the building, the floor, the door itself, all seemed to crackle with anger towards this man who didn't belong.

He lowered his fist. From deep within his person, a voice that shook with overwhelming insistence and overpowering authority rumbled into my ears.

"Do you have the time?" he asked.

Stunned, I looked around, my eyes darting from place to place, searching for the time. I remembered the clock on my stove and looked in the kitchen. The eggs began to smoke, and acrid fumes visibly spread across the room, but all I saw was the time.

"Twelve fifty-one," I said.

"No," he said. "Do you have the time to talk?"

I'd spent years pondering this man and his ways, ages contemplating the nature of his existence, decades dissecting the method to his madness. I'd wondered at his clothing, his origins, and his purpose, delved into the mystery as deep as I could go without venturing into the possible disappointment or madness of the man himself. Now the mystery had come to my doorstep asking to be let in, begging to be solved.

I was petrified. The fun of theorizing had transformed into the terror of the unknown. Who was this man, and why was he here? Why did he want to speak with me? If only I had known the answers before his arrival. If only I had seen the truth of the man before he came to thrust himself upon me. He was not welcome in my home. I did not want to talk.

There was nothing I could do. He asked again, "Do you have the time to talk?"

His raucous voice demanded one answer and one answer only.

"Yes," I said. "Yes, I have the time to talk."

I moved to the side and gestured for him to enter. He took a step into my apartment, and the carpeting filled with static cling at his arrival.

He looked around at my domain. He spotted the couch and sat down, sprawling across the cushions as if he were my sibling, visiting for the hundredth time. The couch began to buzz with a still and empty energy.

I glanced into the hallway to see if anyone had noticed what was going on. Did they see this man knock on my door? Did they see him march into my home with all the authority inherent to a dauntless conqueror? Would they care if he had kicked down my door?

Alas, no soul could be seen. They all had their own business to attend to, their own lives to live, and now the mystery of this man was mine alone to solve.

I closed the door and joined the man seated on my couch.

"I suppose I've only just realized that in all the years I've known you, we've never really spoken. Doesn't that seem strange to you?" I asked the man, straining to veil my discomfort after years of distant, insincere salutations. I could not look him in the eyes.

"No. Nobody speaks to me until I call them. Nobody answers until I knock. It would have been stranger for us to have spoken before now. We may be strangers, but that is not strange at all."

I nodded my agreement. At least this man had some cold logic to explain away my guilt.

"Would you like some eggs?" I asked. "I've got some cooking on the stove."

"No," he replied.

"What about steak? Hash browns? Toast?" Perhaps if I made him feel comfortable, my own discomfort would be somewhat assuaged.

"No. I am not hungry."

"Are you sure? I haven't eaten all day," my stomach groaned from its emptiness.

"Food is the least of our concerns."

The authority with which he spoke stilled my quaking hunger. The discomfort of a vacant stomach paled in comparison to the unwelcome presence of the man seated next to me.

"What exactly would you like to talk about?" I asked, my unease growing by the second. I could not look him in the eyes.

"Nothing," he responded with all the nonchalance of a mobster during a routine shakedown. "Nothing in particular."

"Really? You have no questions for me?"

"None," he said.

"None at all?" I asked.

"None at all."

Bewildered, I racked my brain for any reason he may be here. Perhaps there had been a fleeting comment. Perhaps I'd made an inadvertent invitation. Perhaps I'd nodded twice one day: one nod meant acquaintance, two nods meant friend. No. I'd only ever nodded once, and I'd never said anything to this man, not even a fleeting "hello" or "good day". Damn it, why was he here?

The silence grew too strong.

"Would you mind if I asked you some questions?" I said with a hasty nervousness.

"I suppose not," he replied.

My nerves shook with suspense. At least after all this discomfort, I might gain some answers to the mystery behind this man.

"Where are you from?" I asked, a natural lead.

"A place you haven't heard of, a town you've never been. It doesn't really matter. I'm here now."

A jolt shot through my spine. He was wrong. He had to be.

"You weren't here, not so long ago. You were in the stairwell. You were always in the stairwell. You must like it there. Why else would you have stood there for so long?"

"I stood in the stairwell because that was my place to stand. It belonged to me; it shaped me, and I shaped it. I stood there because I could, but I'm here now."

"Why are you here? You can go back!"

"I can't go back. I'm here now."

Rage began to turn my face red. This man's impertinence had drawn my ire. Who did he think he was? He had forced me to open my door, he had forced me to offer him food, and he had forced me to speak to him. Now he sat on my couch telling me every chance he got that he was on *my* couch in *my* apartment.

I growled at him, "What do you mean, 'you can't go back'?"

"I mean, I'm here now."

I stood up and began to pace. I should not have snapped at him, fury had never lessened his resolve. The man had shown some rationality before, perhaps he would listen to reason now.

"Right, you are here now. However, the stairwell is there now too. Has it grown uncomfortable for you? Are you tired of standing there day in and day out, is that it? If that's the case then you can have my couch. I don't need it, and you seem to like it. You can take my couch, and you can return to the stairwell, and everything will be as good as new, like this never happened," I said, proud of the bargain I had ingeniously devised.

"We can't forget this. We can't work past this. I will not leave. I'm here now."

That was it. That was the last straw. This man had refused to listen to reason, and in my haste to show him my emotion, I turned to where he sat and locked my eyes with his. For the first time in my life, I had looked into the eyes of the man who had stood in the stairwell.

They were cold.

They held within them the contempt of the ancients, a direct opposition to all things new and growing. They possessed a depth that extended further down than the oceans, and a breadth that stretched the world over. His piercing gaze implied the entire universe was subject to his stare; not a single mote or a solitary cell in all existence could escape his sight. His eyes were the window to the void, and I had fallen in.

I collapsed to the ground and shook with tearful tremors. There was nothing to be done. I had been making dinner, and he had knocked. I had nodded on the stairs, and he had come. He was here now.

Through clouded vision, I looked up to see him on the couch. He sat patiently, watching me with those frightful eyes.

"You didn't come to talk," I said, my voice still shaking.

"No," he said. "I came to collect."

I nodded. He was here.

I wiped my eyes and climbed to my feet. With one last nod to the man, I walked to my door and left my apartment, knowing I could never return.

A few doors closed in the hallway around me as I approached the stairwell. Without the man standing there, I could see it like I'd never seen it before. It is there, something that must be seen to be understood. With one last glance back at my old apartment, I descended those eldritch steps, my footfalls echoing with a horrid finality. The apartment, the tenants, the man who would stand, all were behind me as I passed those final steps approaching a door that only opened in one direction. The exit lay before me, and I stepped through.

Now I walk outside the building. I don't know where I'm going, or if I'm going anywhere at all. I only know where I've been, and what I've done. The man who stood in the stairwell for years and years, now lays on the couch in my apartment, feasting on the last meal I'd made for myself. He is there. And now I'm here.

"Are you guys talking in there? Stop it! Wait for me!"

- *Dan Hovseth*

The End

ABOUT AMANDA HOVSETH

AMANDA HOVSETH studied Biblical Studies at New Tribes Bible Institute in Waukesha, WI where she expanded her knowledge of how God has chosen to work in the world and of how unbelievably expansive His love is. She then studied creative writing at the University of Nebraska in Lincoln where she worked in the Writing Center and edited for the Daily Nebraskan.

She now owns and operates Synecdoche Publishing, LLC where she edits, formats, and writes novels.

Her first novel, *Perspective: A Dark Tale of Hope,* can be purchased on Amazon.com.

Follow her on Instagram: @WanderingWillowGifts
Visit her Facebook page: @amandahovseth

ABOUT GILES HOVSETH

GILES HOVSETH lives in Los Angeles, California, where he pursues a career in screenwriting.

He currently works at Parcast where he writes and edits podcast scripts. He also edits and writes for Amanda's company, Synecdoche Publishing LLC.

In his free time, he enjoys writing prose, and his first novella, *Smoldering Ruins,* can be purchased on Amazon.com.

www.ingramcontent.com/pod-product-compliance
Lightning Source LLC
Chambersburg PA
CBHW020659180626
46816CB00003B/1362